About the Author

Karienyia Slonski has always been passionate about writing, athletics, and animals. After earning a degree in the medical sciences, she traveled the world as a gymnastics coach. Her desire to serve at-risk youth and underrepresented populations in the medical and education fields motivated her to complete a Ph.D. She continues to support women's and at-risk populations' causes, serving as a board member of the Living With Grace Fund. She enjoys life in Southwest Florida with her rescue dog and cat, Pippin and Didgeridoo. Her stories reflect both the joys and hardships of life's journey.

She'll be Right

Karienyia Slonski

She'll be Right

Olympia Publishers
London

www.olympiapublishers.com
OLYMPIA PAPERBACK EDITION

Copyright © Karienyia Slonski 2023

The right of Karienyia Slonski to be identified as author of
this work has been asserted in accordance with sections 77 and 78 of
the Copyright, Designs and Patents Act 1988.

All Rights Reserved

No reproduction, copy or transmission of this publication
may be made without written permission.
No paragraph of this publication may be reproduced,
copied or transmitted save with the written permission of the publisher,
or in accordance with the provisions
of the Copyright Act 1956 (as amended).

Any person who commits any unauthorized act in relation to
this publication may be liable to criminal
prosecution and civil claims for damage.

A CIP catalogue record for this title is
available from the British Library.

ISBN: 978-1-80439-069-6

This is a work of fiction.
Names, characters, places and incidents originate from the writer's
imagination. Any resemblance to actual persons, living or dead, is
purely coincidental.

First Published in 2023

Olympia Publishers
Tallis House
2 Tallis Street
London
EC4Y 0AB

Printed in Great Britain

Dedication

I dedicate this book to friends and family who have seen me through good times and bad. Thank you for always supporting my writing endeavors.

Acknowledgements

A special thanks to friends Alexandra, Cindy and Judith, who tirelessly read drafts and encouraged me to publish!

Prologue

I've never had the conversations I needed and probably should have had. Why I didn't isn't a question I can answer. The truth is, I didn't and still don't know how to have those conversations. The meaningful ones – where a simple phrase that wraps a person like a warm, comfy blanket can be recalled when one is confronted with a crisis. The world today doesn't want any more tragedy. At least in my world, it seems the only conversations allowed can be happy ones. Friends, colleagues, and even the bit of family I have wants the mirage that life is all smiles and giggles. Conversations about sunsets, the smell of a newborn baby, puppies, ridiculous dating stories, a new satisfying restaurant – those are the conversations people want. Speaking truth is painful for most of us, and so we don't.

    I am always afraid. I never talked about me – the real me. Hell, I don't even know who that is anymore. Did I ever know? Does it matter? The waltz of life keeps me slightly off-kilter. Thinking that every day may be my last breath helps to justify all those non-conversations. Thank God for the furry creatures comforting me no matter my state of mind. Moments when I did ogle at the sunset, experienced giddiness, expressed innocent and naïve beliefs that someone would pick up the pieces and make it all okay still loom in the abyss. Albeit, those moments seem to have floated so far from my sight. They are like feathers whisked away on the tides going out. Glistening at first, floating with the glorious sunlight touching the feathers' edge until they can no longer be seen.

I often thought about it. I often wondered how I could possibly write about all those things I have chosen to forget. Those non-conversations. I often thought about what part of my life may be even remotely interesting to someone else. But now I am. Writing, I mean. I am willing to share my story – to let others know that life doesn't have to be so hard.

Sitting on the couch in my small, newly built, UK-style home, I can't help to wonder how I got to be here. It seems that I have always been alone, even when people were around me. Life has been a walk through a thorny maze, requiring one band-aid after another, and all the while, I've been afraid to feel any of it. I know now my numbness and mental state of fog were inevitable, but I never imagined they would be haunting me as I near the fifth decade of life.

Growing up in a constant state of fear slowly eroded the outside shell until only the hard, tasteless nut was exposed. The nut was, and probably still is, fear. A fear so visceral that it allowed me to compartmentalize, block out, pretend, and plod through life every day with a painted-on smile.

And here I am – still smiling. While trying to put words on paper, it occurred to me that I must first understand. I have to understand how two people freely came together, had children, and then declared to themselves and those around them that those children never existed. How do you live over fifty years with *that*? It's hard to fathom. How the innocence of babies could lead to the total dismantling of a family – a heritage – a past.

I know that any time a person tries to *really describe* how things are inside at one's core, the knee-jerk reaction is, "Hell, no! As if life isn't hard enough for all of us!" But that's not what this is about. This is about possibility and allowing life to happen. I used to think life happened around me and to me, but never with me. Who knows if that's the case? Who really knows?

Chapter 1

"Quickly! I had to arrange this especially for you. I don't do this favor for everyone. Actually, I have never done this favor, so hurry up. Don't get me in trouble."

"Okay, Okay. I will hurry." With that, I forced myself off the chair in the funeral parlor waiting room. I was terrified someone would see me. Someone who knew me. Someone I knew.

I crept slowly to where she was lying. At first, I didn't recognize her. She was so thin. Not at all like the person I hazily remembered. The gaunt-faced woman who never smiled and clearly enjoyed eating. I didn't know what to expect. I had seen many bodies in the morgue when I worked for the eye bank – but this was different. This was laced with anxiety, fear, and dread of the living. Not the dying.

"I sure don't know if you remember me or know me at all 'cause I sure don't remember you much. I am sorry I don't know you, but how could you have watched and let it happen?" These words I whispered to myself, the whole while subconsciously hoping she would hear and respond. She was my grandmother. My mother's mother. I thought maybe visiting her would give me magical insights. It didn't.

"Hey, you there. Don't forget to sign the guest book at the front."

My deep quiet was broken by the man's voice. I froze instantly. Frozen with fear, I questioned how could I sign the guest book because then they would know I had been here. I couldn't. I wouldn't. I ran out the back of the funeral parlor. The door creaked loudly as it swung shut. Keeping a wild but keen eye on every car approaching the parking lot, I turned the key to my Mustang. It was a few minutes before the funeral home was to open for mourners, and I felt nothing except terror that I may see *her* coming. I laughed out loud at the thought of her mourning her mother like she even gave a shit. I didn't even know if I would recognize my mother if I did see her, but my instinct told me to flee. I ran to the car. It wasn't until I got on the freeway that I heard an audible breath and realized that it wasn't the wind but my own panicked breathing. No one prepared me for this. All I knew was that that was the last shred of concrete proof I existed. Now that tiny shred of fragile existence was going to be buried, and I feared I may never know myself.

With that thought, I tried to cry. But the twenty-six years of numbness and feelings of worthlessness didn't let me. Instead, I could only think, "Is this how it is? You live in a void with no connections to another, and then you die?" I laughed softly at the thought that there was no soap opera moment bringing clarity to this surreal reality.

I arrived at my evening job. My sneaking into a funeral home between visiting hours and seeing my grandmother now seemed all perfectly normal. I knew I could push through, and the earlier day's events would evaporate before my shift was over. I knew it because I practiced pushing my childhood days so far back in my mind on a daily basis. My robotic inner voice kept me moving one step in front of the other. I knew that moving forward and not looking back was the best strategy to live life.

The next morning was sunny and muggy. The humidity was enough to choke a person. Sweat beads started to roll down my forehead within the few minutes it took for me to get to my car.

The damn parking lot was always full at the apartments. I hated having to park at the end of the street because I always worried. A single young woman had to be extra careful. Once I arrived, my boss handed me a phone number I didn't recognize and told me it was a family member. I laughed out loud. Clearly, she had the wrong person. No family members ever called, let alone left messages. Why not? I picked up the phone and dialed before starting my shift. After all, no reason to make some poor stranger wait to find out they had the wrong person.

"Hello, this is Isabella. I think you have the wrong person. Who am I speaking with?"

A high-pitched woman rapidly and pensively spoke on the phone, explaining my grandmother's death. I didn't know this voice. I didn't know this person, but it was made clear I was being invited to some sort of memorial.

"I don't know if I should come." The element of surprise took me with such aghast that I started becoming nauseated. I was sweating. I could feel the instant panic consume me. The fear again paralyzed me.

"I have to think about this. I don't know you. You say you are my aunt? I don't want to take a chance of seeing *her, my mother*."

"Don't be ridiculous. You are Bertha's granddaughter. Your mother won't be here. She thinks she is too good to come back to this neighborhood. Besides, I haven't spoken to your mother for over thirty years, and it seems she is hosting her own funeral memorial at a fancy restaurant. I *am* your aunt, and I am asking you to come. Your grandmother deserves that much."

It took several days for me to decide exactly why my grandmother "deserved that much". I barely knew her, and she certainly did nothing in my lifetime that warranted deserving anything from me. In the end, my curiosity won out. It was the day of the memorial. It took all my courage to get in my Mustang Ghia and make the trip. But I was here. Pulling up to my grandmother's house seemed strange as it was at least twenty-one years ago since I was last there. It was somewhat like I remembered but seemed so tiny and tired-looking on the outside. The bricks on the rowhouse were worn with so many chipped corners that the sand mixture holding it all together was crumbling.

It occurred to me I knew absolutely nothing about her – my grandmother. The one thing I did remember was a cake. She called it a Jewish Apple Cake. I never knew why it was called that, but it was. It was dense with tons of apples in every bite. When we were all allowed to have one at our house, I remembered how I would sneak downstairs and skillfully lift the thin tin cake pan topper so it wouldn't make a noise. Then I would cut the thinnest piece possible because that would be a crime addressed with beatings and placing my hands over the gas stove burner. Walking into her house – Grandma Bertha's house – the taste of Jewish Apple Cake was still with me.

The living room looked stale. Dust was on the furniture, and it was clear no one had bothered to clean up in a while. The air had a stagnant smell. Like the whiff of formaldehyde when I opened the cooler used at my job when I used to work at the eye bank. That smell was familiar to me. The smell of death. Jesus, I just wanted to run out the door. My heart was beating a million times a minute, and I felt a panic attack coming on. "Breathe in and out slowly," I told myself over and over again. The few times I went to this house as a child, I always thought it odd the kitchen was in the basement. This time that thought was one of my first, after which I was assaulted by the wretched smells that accompany old homes where someone just died.

Somehow, I managed to walk down the staircase. That staircase seemed like it was squeezing me and felt more narrow than I remembered. The cocktail chatter of strangers was so deafening that I didn't hear my aunt call my name. I got to the bottom of the steps. As I approached the worn, cracked linoleum landing, a man was sitting in the aged, tweed rocking chair just a few feet from the refrigerator.

Broken bits of memories came back. Who has a chair like that in their kitchen? It is just wrong in every way, I thought. It was the only cloth chair in the kitchen and the tiny, yappy little chihuahua, who I remembered sitting on that chair like it was its throne, was nowhere to be found. Of course, that chihuahua had to have died years ago.

The booming voice of an old man sitting in the chair startled me out of my intense haze of memories. "Who the fuck are you? This is for family! I don't know who you are – get the fuck out – NOW!"

My recoil was so instant. Fear shot through me so uncontrollably I thought I would vomit. The fear was a pain that consumed my body. I could do nothing but stand there. I was frozen. My mind screamed for me to run back up the stairs, but my feet were super-glued to that cracked linoleum. Everyone was staring at me. Their faces were that of horror and confusion. I just stood there feeling helpless – voiceless. I realized my aunt was talking to the stranger in the chair. She was speaking in that loud-like gravely whisper you use in an awkward situation. She started motioning me to come closer to "him" while speaking with firmness and urgency.

"Dad! Calm down! Sit back down! You are going to hurt yourself."

My mind was racing. It was difficult comprehending and processing what my aunt was saying. "Dad?" This is my grandfather! I thought he was dead before I was born. I never recall any mention of him during the short years of my life living with my mother. This must be a mistake.

"This is your granddaughter, Isabella. Dad, please keep your voice down," my aunt urged.

His face was scarred like he had horrible acne in his youthful years. His flat nose was a dead giveaway that he had been a serious alcoholic. Then I noticed the six-pack on the side of the chair, and I felt confident in my assessment of his addiction. Standing there, trying to make sense of this old, belligerent man screaming with insistence for me to leave, was too much. I still couldn't move a muscle. I felt waves of nausea come and go. It was too much. Too much to process. If this was my grandfather – and evidently it was – I had no interest in getting to know him, and it seemed the feeling was mutual.

The man arose again from the chair, this time using a cane. He was a towering, thick-bodied figure which I estimated to be about six-foot-four. His eyes met mine. I stared back at this stranger, still voiceless. He lifted his cane and pointed it at my chest, and said in a very raspy, hoarse but loud voice, "Impossible. You can't be my granddaughter. I only have one grandchild, so get the fuck out!"

Speechless, I stood there, white-faced with hands trembling.

"Dad. This IS your grandchild. This is Kathy's daughter. Kathy has three children. Isabella has a brother and sister." My aunt insisted.

My now grandfather's glare seared through me with such intensity that I felt myself collapse onto the step behind me. Sitting at the bottom of the staircase, he walked two steps toward me and growled, "Kathy is dead. This is for family. Get out!"

I don't remember the minutes after. I don't know how I ran back up the steps and out of that house. My hands were trembling behind the wheel. Fear, numbness, nausea, and anger at myself all enveloped my being at once. I saw a rest stop sign and took the exit. I pulled over and threw the gear shifter into park. What just happened? Breathe, just breathe I told myself. In and out. In and out. I have a grandfather? What the fuck I was ashamed of myself that I allowed myself to be reeled in by my aunt. How could I have been so naïve to consider taking seriously anything anyone remotely related to my mother had to say.

The wave of anger changed to disappointment in myself. Why couldn't I speak up? I was not a child but a young woman who had six years of college behind her. I leaned over and vomited outside the car. I felt better. In the dank rest stop lavatory, staring in the dull mirror that was cracked in three places, I saw the mascara-mixed tears streaming down my cheeks. I didn't cry out loud. I was a master at gathering my emotions and moving forward. I would get through this too. There was no one to tell. Hell, even if I did want to tell a friend, I didn't want pity. No, no – this information had been buried for decades, and so it would stay exactly that – buried.

Chapter 2

"Hey, if it isn't Isabella and her faithful Wadda. Hey girl, you are getting close. D Day is upon us, right? So, last day?"

"Yup, just taking Wadda for her last walk. I see you haven't missed a beat this arvo. What's that, your fourth beer before noon?"

"Correction, it's my fifth, but who's counting. Right, Wadda? Tell your mom that life isn't always about chasing rabbits and herding sheep."

Looking at Scottie, I vowed that I would never end up back here in the bush. The endless sand beach sometimes felt like it could swallow me up, and no one would miss me. Well, Wadda would. Wadda and Stevie. Maybe even the garage dweller who sold the odd boomerang during season. Not once did the old man offer Wadda a boomerang despite years of "g'days". This was a vast wasteland of belligerent asshole swizzy with little to no ambition. Work, drink, work, drink, repeat. In between work and drink, sex – of course.

In my short fifteen years and nine months of living, I already sensed people were full of shit. I had a keen intuition for the bad penny. The ones that looked good on the outside like a beautifully sculpted pomegranate with thick glittery skin and mysterious ruby red sections. Then, you open up that pomegranate and find out it's all bruised, with dark rotten flesh and sour inside. Thank God I was leaving West Australia behind, and it couldn't come any quicker. Funny, really, how little I thought about the actual act of leaving, and now it was here. Twenty-four hours before I got on a plane to America. Gonna miss these big ole boulders. I thought about the number of days wasted chasing goannas, spying on galar nests, and watching the kangaroos graze on the golf course.

"So… Isabella, you ready? Better start packing your warm clothes. No boardies and bare feet for you for the next six months. Can't forget it's gonna be Fall and Winter there. Where you going again? Pennsylvania?"

"Very funny, Scottie. Good try. No, I am going to Maryland. Do you ever listen to anything I ever say? I've been walking Wadda past your house for eight years now so I expect you to check in on Wadda. Can you do that for me?"

"Yup, no worries matey. I take it Stevie won't? Selfish narcissist. So, how's pineapple man taking all this? You are gonna be a great doctor one day. Well I'll tell you this, Maryland doesn't know who's coming to take them by storm."

"Very funny. And I'm sure *pineapple man* is going to be devastated – not. Every time I think about his last foodie truck and how I backed it up into the main city water pipe! Hysterical! Too bad he didn't think so. His fault though, I told him I didn't have a license yet. The water gushed like a fire hydrant going wildly out of control. It was the most exciting event at that miserable little fair. All the little kids jumped around in the gushing flow of water like little nutters. What a site. But, what did he care about? Me? The vehicle? Nope. Just the profit made selling his bloody pineapple fruit sticks! How can love ever compete with that? Those fruit kabobs were genius and he sold them like the Rolling Stones sold CDs."

"Well, he's older than you, but my guess is you outsmart him at every turn. Not every kid goes across the world to college at fifteen by themselves. I couldn't even make it out of Cottasloe, but I'm no worse for it. Good luck to you though!"

"I'm gonna miss you, Scottie. Be gentle with all those tinnies you toss back. Try to keep it down to a minimum of two before noon. You know, every tourist spends a lifetime saving to get here – well not here, here in the bush, but to see the Great Coral Reef, the koalas, Crocodile Dundee, Steve Irwin's legacy blah blah blah. I don't get it. There's a lot more to see in the world – I'm sure."

The MG came tearing around the bend fishtailing in the soft Sandy road. How I loved that old fixer-upper, but even more than the MG, I loved Stevie. He was never going to be my knight in shining armor – as if there is such a thing. Hard to believe so many women get bamboozled by that bullshit. I wasn't stupid or that naïve.

Meeting Stevie was destiny. I was sure of it. He was six-foot-two. Either confident or delusional, as he was sure he was destined to be running for Parliament before the end of earning his Master's Degree in political science. Only one more year, and he would be canvassing the neighborhood, poising himself to become the next Mister Margaret Thatcher. I would be done with my pre-med studies by the time he was ready to start campaigning. It would be perfect.

"Hey Stevie, you chewing it with my Sheila here? I came to steal her away. It's our last day together before she flies into the big blue sky. Rides off into the wild, wild West."

"Here she comes now. Poor Wadda. I don't know whose gonna miss the other more. My bet is on Wadda."

"Hey, you two!" We had just finished our final race after bungarras. "Sorry, Wadda, but mama's gotta leave you, but tonight you and Stevie and I will take one more look from Rock

Mountain! Let's get going, Stevie. Times ticking."

"Hey, Isabella…don't y'all forget to write, ya hear? Isn't that what the Seppos say – damn Americans. Be careful around them! Seems they can be a bit egomaniacal. By the way, you are wrong. Most people save up their whole lives to get to Hawaii. Evidently a luau with tiny-hipped women doing the hula while getting smashed until they wake up the next morning in the sand is preferred over an Australia holiday. Then they realize they just cheated on their spouse. That is what all people save up for their whole lives.

"Okay, Scottie, I see your cynicism reigns again. Better than the pub jokes though. One can only imagine the 'seeing eye dog being twirled around above the blind guy to check out the women' so many times sober. A classic! You know, we can't all be that lucky to make jokes from tag lines on BBC and Public Broadcasting. You go real deep for sure! Cheers, matey. Don't worry – I'll never forget you!"

Getting into the dark, olive green MG with the shaggy torn edge of the rag top was never easy for Wadda. With no real back seat, Wadda had to scrunch up half on me and half in the small space behind the front seat. But Wadda never seemed to mind. Just wagged her tail, oblivious that this would be her last night with me in the bush. I wasn't coming back.

"So, Isabella, Rock Mountain?" Stevie said as he ground the gear into first.

"What do you think, Wadda? Yup, Wadda agrees – Rock Mountain! Bye, Scottie!" With that, I rolled up the window to keep the dust at a minimum.

The winding sandy road was always a challenge for the MG. It was like the little train that could, or should I say, the little MG that tried. The hour drive to the top was not nearly enough time to dream about all the possibilities ahead. Hell, my sister left me in the lurch when I was twelve, my bother when I was fifteen, and if it weren't for Mom and DAD "D" rescuing me from a cesspool of parental dysfunction, I would have probably wound up an addict or worse.

"Whalla whoo! It's a spectacular view from here, Isabella. I don't know how you are going to leave this!" The mountain was dotted with sharp black and white edges, blackboy trees, and tall pines. The thickness of the smell of surf salt filled my senses. "I know you, Queen Nature Shaman. You are going to be lonely without tons of animals around you. I just can't get over it – you are going to be a real city girl. Hey, I have a surprise for you."

"Stevie, I'm flattered. Surprised! It's so unlike you. Wow, a classic red plaid blanket, basket filled with brie and Shiraz, olives and mozzarella. Hmmmm, seems like all the things you like. Brilliant, mate. What a way to show how much you will miss me!"

"Now hold on, Isabella. I took a lot of time to prepare this for you. You know I love you. You are the only girl who challenges me! For Christ's sake, you are going to college at fifteen and taking not one, but two majors on a scholarship."

"Half scholarship. And I am not sure about two majors. I am going to need to figure out how to pay the rest. I will have to find housing too. But such flattery gets you everywhere. And I will be sixteen my second month of college. I figure someone has a gymnastics studio where I can get a coaching gig. I can teach riding lessons to all those little rich kids too. It will be a new adventure and a clean slate. Not one person will know my story, so it's a win-win, no matter what I have to do to make it there."

"You need to let loose a bit and give yourself permission to admit you are scared shitless. You are wound so tight most of the time, Alice in Wonderland's time keeper. Do you ever let go? Doesn't anything ever make you feel? Feel sad? Nervous? If we could bottle up your coping skills and sell it, we would be instant millionaires. That's what I love about you. Doesn't matter how much shit gets thrown at you, you smile and see that half full glass. Lucky for you, I know there is one thing that I know can make you euphorically happy."

Stevie's soft kisses sent me reeling. Well, that and the Shiraz. So unfair to other girls that that this gorgeous specimen of a man was mine – all mine. A top Division One rugby player, College Valedictorian, a 5.0 tennis player, and in love with me. Hard to believe! Getting wet uncontrollably anticipating his kisses and knowing in one thrust I will reach euphoria.

"Hey, Isabella! Are you with me here? What are you thinking about?" Stevie's eyebrows narrowed hinting of impatience and frustration. Forget it, I'm trying to get close to you and make you feel special. Should have known that was impossible. You have to be the oldest minded teenager I know. It's like being around a thirty-year-old woman sometimes with you."

"What? Wait a minute – what do you know about thirty-year-old women?"

Just then, Stevie stopped touching me and pulled slightly away. He looked down at the water flowing below the mountain. When he lifted his face, the light gave away his secret. Something was up.

"What did I say?" I asked with sincerity.

"Nothing. Just that crack about the thirty-year-old women. I know you mean my boss. Why are you jealous? Not to say that I didn't think about it. Can we forget her?"

The way the light danced on his forehead when he lifted his head revealed his smirk. It was then I knew.

"Oh no, no, no, no! You didn't! You wanker! You piece of shit! You fucked your boss? I should have known!"

"Isabella, don't be ridiculous. Yes, my boss comes on to me but, I–I–I never."

The rest seemed like a blur. Like one of those movie scenes where a blizzard sweeps across the mountain plains. I envisioned a young girl screaming for her husband and baby to make it to the shelter, and no matter how hard she tried, she didn't make it. The avalanche slides, and the husband and baby are swept away under the cold blue-hued mounds of snow.

"Wadda! Come on girl, get in the car. I love you so much – Wadda – not you Stevie. I can't wait to get out of this shit hole of a town."

Grabbing the four corners of the hideous red plaid blanket, the makeshift sack littered the shiraz bottle as I rushed, stumbling on the tiny graduated brown pebble stone-sand mixture to the MG. With the glass smashed into little bits, I could only think about hoping Wadda didn't cut her paws while trying to lick the brie off the ground. That bastard! How could he? How could she? She is twice my age!

The tension in the MG going back down Rock Mountain into Wallaroo was unbearable. The sun went down behind the mountain, and even Wadda was restless from the tension between us. The romantic send-off was obviously a bust. Nothing like knowing it's really over before I even got to the other side of the globe. Better to avoid telling the two friends I had growing up here. I didn't need an "I told you so" or a "Be glad he showed his colors now rather than waiting four years and fantasizing about being together." Seriously, we all *know* those clichés, but nobody wanted to hear it come from anyone else's lips. I could just imagine a voice in slow motion speed like an old record player put on the wrong speed saying, "I told you so." I couldn't help myself. The absurdity of the whole thing. Just the image made me laugh out loud.

"What is so funny? I never meant to hurt you. Look, you are going away, and you are young. I love you, but it's not like I am *in love* with you. You gotta be smart enough to know that…right?"

"So, you thought I was a sad, lonely damsel in distress the past two years that you needed to rescue? And all the while I thought you were attracted to my great legs, witty quips and disappoint. I actually thought it was possible that someone could love me!"

"You have your whole life ahead of you. You are going across the world and within a few months you will totally forget all about me. I promise. Guys will be dying to be with you."

"Oh, is that what you are trying to tell yourself? You don't want to burden me with your selfless love you bestowed upon me? Get a grip. You banged your boss, and I don't fit in your ambitious campaigning profile. She must, though. I get it. No one wants the girl who is damaged goods with a psychotic mother and a wimp of a father."

"C'mon, Isabella. That's not what I'm saying. I am just saying you have a big life ahead of you and I have a plan. You don't fit the kind of image I am going to need. I love you, and I want you to be happy, but I can't give you what you need. Trust me, you are gonna thank me one day."

The tears didn't stop until well into the early morning hours. Exhausted and heartbroken, I had two hours to pack and get to the airport. There weren't going to be any loving family memories of a grand send-off. There weren't going to be any family portraits to frame, hang on walls, or put on bookshelves.

There weren't going to be any good luck banners or care packages or a surprise goodbye.

The taxi honked. It was time to move on. I could do this. Besides Wadda, no one was saying goodbye. There was nothing for me to take that I wanted. Gymnastic medals, tennis and sailing trophies, and netball awards were only memories, as I was sure they were thrown in the trash when I left to stay with Mom and Dad D. But I did pack the cricket bat – you never know when that will come in handy. I heard stories about the crazy gun owners in America, so you can never be too careful.

With my rucksack and cricket bat, I looked back at the little room at Mom and Dad D's, where I spent the past few years on and off. Thank God for them. I knew their kids were relieved that I was leaving, as being an extra in the house wasn't exactly making everybody happy. Mom and Dad "D" wanted to be there but taking time off from work was not an option for either of them. I was okay with that as I knew I would always be in their hearts. It was time. No one was there, but Wadda for the big send-off. "That's it, Wadda. You take care old girl. I love you!"

Reaching the airport departing lane, I felt a lump in my throat. This was really it. Check-in, buy gum, get some chocolate and find a seat at the terminal. I was ready. The adrenaline was running overtime, and my hands were slightly shaky when I handed the plane ticket to the stewardess. It was going to be a long flight. Twenty-nine hours in the air to sleep, watch bad movies, eat, change planes, and try to pretend I wasn't alone. The plane started down the runway. I watched from the window and marveled at how quickly what was below disappeared. Like I never existed here in the first place. Nope, I was never coming back.

Chapter 3

Sitting in the cloth-covered metal chair in the third row, I listened to the university president's welcome speech to all the graduates. I was devoid of emotion. With my black, gold-edged cap and gown and Kelly green sash draped around my neck, I could barely manage a smile. I was so, so tired. The journey was long and hard. I could barely believe it myself, really – that I pushed through and made it to graduation. In fact, all I could muster up was how, in the end, graduating from college was not all that significant in my life. Besides my classmates' families, there was no one there to cheer for me when it would be my turn to walk across the stage. I looked up at the sunny, blue sky dotted with cumulus clouds that collided together, looking like off-kilter angel wings. I stared at the sky for a while, deep in thought.

Actually, I almost missed the graduation ceremony all together. My boss at the newspaper obituary desk asked me to come and work. The fact that she even asked seemed to underscore the insignificance of graduating from college. I reminded her I was graduating the day before, but she knew I needed the money and was easy to persuade. I don't know why I could never say "no". I said I would work unless she had found someone else. At the last second, my boss called and told me she found someone else. I wound up going to the graduation ceremony after all.

My doubts about being surrounded by a sea of strange well-wishers were confirmed when I arrived and took my place in the sixth seat in the third row of the endless row of metal chairs. I was still a nothing. That's how I felt. Despite finishing Cum Laude graduate with pre-med and speech and language pathology courses behind me, I didn't feel like I *made* it. I came in almost sixteen and left feeling a hundred. Simple as that. Finally, my name was called. When I approached the stage, it felt like only a brief reprieve from a torrential downpour. It was a momentary blip of solace, like when the green grass blades glisten from raindrops, and the sun peeks out from behind a cloud. It was just another moment of another day of many, many days.

When I first entered the university, I didn't even declare a program under my major of pre-med. Who knows what they want when they are barely sixteen? Especially when one comes alone to a new country and has to house, feed, and clothe oneself? I only knew I wanted to be a gymnastics coach or a physical education teacher. Neither of these were an option at this university. I was granted a tennis and academic scholarship, but it only covered half the tuition. Hell, it didn't even provide me a meal plan. Tennis wasn't a huge sport in the Jesuit-run university, but I liked the mascot of a greyhound. I loved sports. I loved animals. Pre-med was my declared major, but more than that was too much to think about. It never occurred to me I had to pick a *program*. Unfortunately, the program for which I signed up was a mistake – the result of a fifteen-second conversation between myself and another.

I recalled that conversation like it was yesterday. During the campus tour, a college advisor asked what I enjoyed in life as she noticed I didn't pick a program. I distinctly remember saying I liked kids and sports. She smiled, took my hand, and guided me to a clinic across the campus. Through a two-way viewing window, I watched a doctor work with an infant who had a tube inserted below its belly button. She told me the tube was the infant's source of nutrition. I asked what major that doctor took, and the advisor answered, "Speech and Language Pathology." Right then and there, I said, "Sign me up."

After the four years I spent studying the profession, I knew I hated speech pathology and wanted to get on with life. I took the medical school entrance exams and did well, but there was no money, and I had to keep living. During the last four years, I tired of people and their drama. The constant bullshit. Having to make my bosses, tennis coaches, and professors happy, combined with the energy vampires of immature college students and pseudo-friends, was too much. It took its toll; I swore off humans. Thank God for my cat, Suki, at the end of every day. My passion for helping animals would have to wait. Looking back now, I realize what a dim wit I was! The truth was, I could have studied four years deconstructing an ant's ass, and I would have just pushed through and gotten "A"s so I would earn a degree.

I knew from birth I had to go to college. It was never a *choice*. At five, I remember being forced to stand out on the front concrete stoop, brushing my hair and reciting the times' tables. *She* was there. It was a daily ritual. One wrong answer – and the eights and nines always tripped me up – and a fist would slam into the midsection of my back. "You are so stupid. Do it again. You aren't getting into college if you can't say your times tables'." Funny, maybe she was right, because I had to drop my statistics class in Sophomore year at university. It was the only class in which I have ever gotten an "F". I remember the wave of devastation and humiliation when I got the mid-term back. The teacher announced there were only two "A"s, and I was sure one was mine. It wasn't. I got an "F". No, I earned an "F". I cried and agonized for a week. I finally decided to go to the registrar's office and drop the course. I had no energy or time left to devote to statistics. I failed. I was a failure.

The words of the university president flowed in one ear and out the other. I was deep in thought. His light-hearted joke about the freshman fifteen sent my mind reeling. There was never any fear that I would gain the famous "freshman fifteen". I rarely ate two meals on any one day, and there was no shortage of exercise in my life. Tennis team practice required four hours every day. I worked the graveyard shift, taking eyes or corneas from corpses three days a week at the eye bank. I wrote obituaries for the Baltimore major newspaper two days a week and every weekend, and coached gymnastics four times a week. I studied during my jobs, in between my jobs, and after my jobs. Playing tennis felt like a fourth job, and I rarely had the strength to win matches or the peace of mind to allow me to focus. I was good at tennis but knew I would never be the next Chris Evert.

Fucking Hallelujah! My name was called, "Isabella Notski." I got up and looked around. As I approached the stage, the whooping and hollering for the student before me was beginning to subside. No one cheered my name. I heard a few pity claps by professors. Exiting the stage, my urge to run to my car and leave university behind forever was squelched by a familiar voice saying, "Go, Notski!" Back in my seat, I turned my head, straining to find the face that belonged to the familiar voice. Finally, I locked eyes with my "on again, off again" boyfriend, Jan, who was standing next to the graduate's family welcome table. He gave me the thumbs-up sign, forced a tiny smile, and walked away toward the exit path of campus.

It felt like an eternity listening to the remainder of graduate names. Finally, it was over! It was a relief in so many ways. I had enough time to take a nap before going to coach and then work at the eye bank. I walked for the last time past the large cherry blossom trees that lined the entrance to the chapel on the campus. I smiled and waved when a few classmates caught my attention and continued on with their families and friends. Walking on the path, I recalled the second week of school during Theology class when the Jesuit stated that going to church was not mandatory. God would still love us. That was the last time I, and I think the rest of my classmates, went into that chapel on campus for any type of prayer service.

I walked past the white stone library and began the ascent up the slope to the lesser-used parking where I parked my car. The smell of the gardenias lining the pathway filled my senses and reminded me of the sweet victory of winning my last university tennis match. Jan met me off the court with a fist full of gardenias that match! At least I had *that*.

The path was long and boasted pink and purple clovers that hosted an infinite number of bees. I passed the dormitories and entered the extra sports practice field bordered by the parking lot and a row of neighborhood houses that were separated from the campus by a metal chain link fence. I found myself chuckling when I thought about that fence and a little black and white terrier. We were running flag football plays for a charity game for Santa Claus Anonymous. I was supposed to catch the pass. While running down the very muddy field, out of the corner of my eye, I saw a dog jump the fence and tear across the field. To this day, I'm positive he just wanted to play ball too. Just as I leaped upward to catch the football, I felt this sharp, quick pain sear through my calf. I dropped the ball and fell to the ground. An Aussie playing football was a bit of stretch – the terrier made his point. He grabbed the ball and ran across the field while I was left butterflying the dog bite on my calf. I didn't have the time or money to go get stitches, a butterfly bandage would have to do.

When I got to my car, I turned and stopped. I took one last look. Hard to believe that the culmination of all that work came down to this moment. A single, silent moment in an asphalt parking lot by myself. I opened the white door and sat in the burgundy-red leather seat. I had been having trouble with the transmission lately. If my car could just hang in there a little longer until I get to work, I would be grateful. That's all I could ask – I earned that much.

Chapter 4

"Crikey mate. This is cool! So, you are telling me that you can hook me up to JJJ Australia radio channel from here?"

"Sure can, little woman. Howard told me to expect a pretty little Aussie ,and I am guessing you are she. I am the master of all music here at WR Royal University Radio. Savor the Flavor is my newest program. So would love to hook into new tunes. Happy to pay homage to U.K. artists! I know it's not going to be long before we have a big global surge of radio frequencies through a computer. But right now, having global radio access is an advantage of this job."

My first thought was, "Not another crunchie granola," but I was glad that Howard introduced me to the university radio station and hooked me up with the station manager. Honestly, when I entered the musty basement, I wasn't expecting much. I felt like I was going to choke from the overpowering, pervasive mold smell. Clearly, the Jesuits didn't think modern music; well, any music, was a priority.

"So, what's your vibe? Rock and roll? Heavy metal? hip hop? God forbid, disco crap? I am Ryk with a "Y", by the way, in case you didn't know."

"Well, Ryk, with a Y, if you must know, I saw the German band Rammstein in concert. By your facial expressions, I am guessing you probably haven't heard of them. You can't get any more heavy metal than that, but I only went for the light show! It takes over fifty pyro tech specialists to put on their concert."

"That's rad, yeah, that's rad. You have some kind of accent, but I got you. I'm sure you heard that before."

"Yup. By the way, I also like techno. I love music festivals. Are there any here?"

"Oh, yeah baby. I'll introduce you to my friends. We are meeting up at campus pub tonight. You in?"

"Tonight? I'd love to…but I gotta go make the bacon mate. But goodonya on the invite. Another time maybe? Y-y-you still go to college here? You seem, well, too old for college. You manage the radio station, right?" I stammered and rambled on, a bit embarrassed for asking.

"Oooookay, I'll take that as a compliment? Here's the scoop. I am a bit old to be finishing, but I got this small thing going on."

Ryk pulled his badly pilled grey sweater sleeve up over his forearm and revealed a place for vascular access dialysis. Clearly, he had some issues as he was drinking a beer in the afternoon. To walk a step in another's shoes quickly came to mind. Looking at the scarred tracks of veins called for empathy. Growing up around medicine definitely gave me an edge. I've seen arteriovenous fistulas before. Frightening when first looking at them. Looking at the egg-sized mounds of flesh popping up along Ryk 's veins was no pretty sight. It called for engaging in a truly scientific observation and dissection strategy to ignore the fact that the arm was grotesque by anyone's standards.

"Oh buggar! I'm sorry. So, you are dialysis dependent? That fistula closest to your wrist looks like it could use some infection control."

"Oh, so now you are a dialysis nurse? Don't need another. I got enough of them. Why do you think I hide down here at the music station? No complaints. I've the best of both worlds – education and music."

I surveyed Ryk while he continued ad nauseam talking about his take on U.K. bands. He wasn't the worst-looking guy; blond hair, green eyes, a bit pudgy and shorter than me. Being five-foot-nine wasn't the easiest when it comes to dating, so I wondered if it's an obstacle for short guys. Being athletic and tall had its drawbacks too. My wide shoulders and big bone frame begets the comment, "You a swimmer or football player?" I never saw myself as having good looks or a great body. I know I had muscle; after all, I trained over thirty hours a week trying to make the regional and national gymnastic teams until a severe injury at twelve. After which, I turned to tennis. Then it was all about tennis.

Leaving the room, I turned and winked at Ryk. "See ya, matey!" Figured I'd throw him a bone because the one lesson I had down pat about life was social capital is useful. Never hurts to have more likes than non-likes.

"Hope so. I mean you seem like a cool cat. If you are ever lonely, we can always put shrimp on the barbie." Ryk smirked a bit when sharing his stereotype knowledge.

"Haha. Music Ryk. You did *not* just call me a cool cat. What are you, fifty? See ya around and thanks for adding JJJ to your Savor the Flavor programming!"

Checking my watch as I made my way back down the damp, moldy-smelling basement hallway, I couldn't wait to get back to civilization and breathe fresh air. I had just four minutes to run across campus and make biology class.

"Oh crap, I left my damn text book in the car." I heard myself mutter out loud a few yards from the lecture hall. Just at that moment, someone rushed by, hitting my elbow. Things went flying. Could I ever get a break?

"Hey, hey, I'm so sorry."

Kneeling on the mulch bed below the cherry blossom tree, grabbing my disheveled notebook and loose ditto papers, a wave of frustration hit me. For one brief second, I thought I may tear up. Then I looked into this glorious man's face!

It's him! The guy I was weirdly but strongly attracted to during tennis practice. He's never said hi to me. He always looked away whenever I looked at him. I figured he must have a girlfriend. "Oh my God. I'm so sorry. I'm late for my class and was rushing. Let me help you."

"Yeah. I know the feeling – the rushing from place to place. I try to be on time though. Thanks for that."

Still helping me to gather the white papers with illegible handwriting, Jan looked at me. Really looked.

"Uh, I'm Jan. Hey, aren't you on the tennis team? I'm sorry, but I don't know your name."

Of course, he didn't. Filled with awe, I felt like the first time I ever drove through a car wash and watched the endless bubbles and hula skirt-like leather straps lather up the car. I was befuddled but pleasantly surprised. This guy was talking to *me*.

"Your name?"

"Oh! I'm Isabella. It's not often I'm at a loss for words." I blushed.

"Nice to meet you –formerly, that is – Isabella. I noticed you have a great forehand and a solid serve. What do you clock at?"

Blushing, I wanted to crawl back into a hole. I never "clocked" my serve as I didn't want to admit I probably fell short compared to my teammates. All I could muster for a reply was, "Crikey, I'm now late. Dr. Ridge is a stickler."

"I remember old Ridge. Ball buster for sure. Doesn't let one thing slip. I took his class three years ago, but if you ever need help, I'm going to be hanging out at the UPub tonight. You should come. I can introduce you around."

Running with papers barely stabilized in my over-stuffed binder, I started to walk away. "Can't, gotta work. See you on the court though."

When I entered the lecture hall, it was so quiet you could hear students breathing in rhythmic unison. Dr. Ridge looked up with a scowl and called me out. What a knob. Was it really necessary – the dickwad.

"Ms. Notski, nice of you to join us. This is not a long-distance learning class."

My brain immediately retorted, "Please! You can't think of something more original?" I just smiled and sat down. I was doing well in this class and wanted to keep an "A" so didn't want to disrespect Dr. Ridge. Since most all the professors were Jesuits with Ph.Ds in their field, students treated the professors with a high level of respect. I said, show me *why I* should respect you. Sarcasm like that didn't push the respect meter to the top in my book.

Coming out of class, my brain was numbed by a plethora of information. Surviving on chocolate milk with ice and a snickers bar for breakfast and lunch didn't help my academic or work performance. I decided during bio class I would ask for another day working at the obit desk this month. I could use the money for more nutritious food. Tennis matches will be over. The end of October was only two weeks away.

Opening the oversized solid mahogany doors of the lecture hall and walking into the grand marble-lined hallway, I heard my name.

"Hey, Notski."

To my left was Jan sitting inside the huge arched window lined with a three-foot mahogany sill. I waved and walked over.

"Hey, you waiting for me?"

"Well, sort of. I figure I can walk you back to the car. The least I can do after causing you to be late for bio. I'm headed home and a young girl can never be too careful these days."

"Well, since you put it that way. Can never be too careful. So, what's your story, mate?"

"I've got to finish this semester and then I'll be going to dental school. I'm Polish. I came here with my parents when I was thirteen so interpreting is my unpaid job. I've been living with my parents, but I signed a lease today near the dental school downtown. I move during Christmas break in time to start Spring semester at John's Hopkins school of dentistry. What about you? I am guessing you live off campus with no dorm sticker on your windshield. I also am guessing you are not from around here."

"Yup, you are a regular sleuth, aren't you? I'm from West Australia and taking pre-med and speech and language pathology. I work a ton, and usually I'm like a jackrabbit running from school to work, to my other work, and then back to school to study.

While walking to the parking lot, Jan shared his plight with the various Jesuits here. It was good to know who to avoid since he took all the pre-requisites I needed to take. Insider information on professors and classes is always a plus when signing up for the upcoming semester. We got to the parking lot. Jan followed me to my car.

"Here I am. This is me."

"Nice Ghia. I'm right over there. The VW bug. My Dad is a master VW mechanic."

"Go figure. My gear shifter isn't working well. Think he can look at it?"

"I don't see why not. Happy to help out. How about

tomorrow late in the afternoon?"

"Uh, let me check my schedule. I gotta skedaddle." I slipped into the Ghia front seat.

"The day after tomorrow? Or the day after that?"

I shook my head and mouthed "working" through the front windshield. I read about the mouthing technique in a romance novel and was under the impression it would create a sexy effect. Oddly, what I really wanted to do was jump in his arms and have him hold me tightly until tomorrow.

Jan took out a notebook page and wrote his name and number and placed it under my windshield wiper. Then he slapped another note on the driver's side window with the words, "Your number?"

I motioned I would call him using the universal hand signal of pinky to mouth and thumb to the ear. I opened the window and reached out to remove Jan's notes. The gear shifter ground the car into reverse, and I backed out. Once on the turnpike, I thought about how signs like "up yours," "hang tight," "a-okay," and the ultimate middle finger of "piss off" worked in every country. Done overanalyzing hand symbols, I turned my focus to when I would call him. I had Jerzy's number! I still had no rationale for why I was attracted to him. He didn't boast of a sharp-edged Greek god sculpted face but had kind eyes. Blue-green eyes with wavey hair about an inch above the collar.

He walked with the confidence that said, "I rock." On the court, I'd watched him shake hands with his opponent in such a manner that his body exuded the message "…And now I'm going to kick your ass." His tennis record was legendary. He had not lost one match, not one, since his freshman year. He was like the God of the Courts. I still couldn't believe I had his number. He was intense. When he looked at a person, his eyes said, "I *see* you," like some kind of mystic who knew there was more behind a person's eyes than they cared to admit.

Work and school were uneventful over the next week. The last tennis match was in one week, and my win record was shameful at best. I had to demonstrate my worth and knew that "no excuses" had to be my motto. I was determined to win and prove I was worthy of the scholarship. Coach knew I was burning numerous ends of numerous candles, and he had been cutting me slack. I owe this final win to him and the team. I've never been much of a team player. All my sports have essentially been individualistic within a team. The phrase "being a team player" always conjured up the image of Snoopy for me for a reason with which I could relate. Snoopy was a lovable loner but participated when a critical moment of team-ness was necessary. I definitely could see myself in Snoopy. Tomorrow was another day, and I would finally have time to reach out to Jan. I hoped his interest had not waned. Smiling to myself, I recited my daily mantra, "things are great and tomorrow will be better", before going to bed. I totally believed in sending positive energy to the universe. The day was a lot crispier after the word crispier, add the phrase: than expected at the end of September. Outside than I expected when I rolled out of bed and opened the door. I was feeling very fortunate I had this apartment. I already moved twice since I landed in the US, as each place I found increased the rent after my first month, forcing me to move. This was a God send. This apartment was perfect. Ten minutes from the university and on the top floor. It was an old red-brick row home at Fells Point. The inside left much to be desired, and the neighborhood was a bit questionable – eclectic for sure. The apartment living room view was the hill of some great battle at Fort McHenry. I thought that one of these days, I'll check out the monument sign and find out what that battle was about. But now, I was going to call Jan.

I punched the numbers on the phone. Part of me hoped he wouldn't answer. The other part of me wanted nothing short of him answering. Three rings, four rings, bingo!

"Ah, G'day, is Jan there?"

My ears were met with something unintelligible, and I realized it was someone speaking in Polish. That person didn't understand me, and I didn't understand the speaker. I repeated his name, "Jan. Is Jan there?"

The voice trailed off, and suddenly Jan was speaking. "Hello, Can I help you?"

"Jan, it's me, Isabella." Feeling slightly awkward, I rambled on about tennis, how I needed to win, and how his serve was awesome and mine sucked. I finally got around to the point, circumlocution was my strength, "So, can you meet me at the tennis court later this arvo – ah, this afternoon – and help me out? I finally have some time off."

"Yeah, yeah. I mean, YES! Maybe you can just drive over to my house, and I can have my Dad look at your car. Then we can drive to the courts in my car. What do you think?"

My first reaction was to say "no." I didn't need any favors. I could take care of myself. Jan must have sensed my hesitation because then I heard, "Are you there? Not too much too soon, is it?"

"No, I am just not used to people being nice to me and offering to help for free."

"No big deal, really. Hold on, he's right here. I'll ask him."

Listening to the very glottal language of Polish, I wondered what they were actually talking about because it seemed like an eternity of dialogue. Either that or everything in Polish required significantly more words than in English. But I definitely sensed it wasn't just about cars.

"Okay, we are set. My address is 2626 Fodder Lane. You can come by at three, and my Dad will check out your car. Does that work for you?"

"Yes! That's perfect! You rock, matey. I will see you later! Cheers!"

The mound of reading I had for school was immense. I had about five hours before I had to leave for Jan's. I turned on the radio and tuned into Royal University. Son of a bitch if I didn't hear indigenous music from the Australian group "Warumpi Band". It was Savor the Flavor hour.

"I'm pumping the jam this afternoon. If you didn't already know, this is your host, Ryk with a "Y". This next tune I am dedicating to a little Aussie lady. It's electronic rock genre from this next group, Regurgitator, recently featured at the music fest Big Day Out. Enjoy, Isabella, enjoy!"

The day went by quickly. Too quickly. There wasn't enough time in the day. I looked in the mirror. I didn't look too bad. Not too preppy, not too sexy. Who was I kidding? "Sexy?" I don't even know what that means with my "moose" of a body! I threw on a ribbed, navy blue turtleneck, a pair of jeans with a flower patch on the right knee and an open tear on the left knee, and red suede boots. Mom "D" always said I was at my best from the ankles up due to my very fat and flat feet. I was glad it was cold out, and I could keep Jan from being visually assaulted by my ugly feet. I grabbed my tennis bag, sweats, and cup of tea and was out the door.

Weaving through cobble-stoned roads, I finally came to 2626 Fodder Lane. I was a bit nervous. I felt the pit of my stomach turn and churn a few times. I was grateful the car would be checked out. It was rusting at the bottom of the driver's side door, and I was sure the chassis had rusted as well. I sensed the clutch wasn't going to hold out much longer either.

The house stood alone with an attached garage. It looked like it sat on two lots and a VW sign was over the second garage-type building on the property. Jan waved as I pulled into the driveway and motioned me to pull the car up to the garage door of the second building.

"Hey, Isabella. Glad you could make it. This is my Dad, Nicholai."

"Hello, Ms. Isabella. My son say car need help?"

"So nice to meet you Mr. Nicholai. Yes! Yes! Something is very wrong with the gear shifter, and I think the clutch needs work. It doesn't seem to want to go into gear, and it makes this awful grinding noise."

"Uh, okay, let me translate for Dad."

A short exchange between Jan and his Dad, and Jan got in the Ghia and drove it into the garage. Looking at Nicholai's teeth, I could see why Jan wanted to be a dentist.

"My Dad said you need new tires. You really can't be driving around in the winter storms with those bald tires. Not safe at all. Come on in and meet my mom."

"Yeah, I know I need tires, but I only have so much money – a girl has to eat! Oh, I don't know. Meet your mom, too? Really? Now?"

"Why not? She is making some perogies."

I followed him into his house and wondered what perogies were. Entering the living room, I took my boots off and was greeted with an athletic, slim blue German Weimaraner. The room smelled of cooking, but the scent of the cuisine eluded me. I never was much of a foodie, and I considered myself – as did every person I have ever eaten with – a plain Jane. Some called it "too picky".

Still petting the beautiful Weimaraner, Jan joined in.

"Her name is Kera Sha."

I knelt down and gave Kera a few moments to get used to me. I scratched around her ears, and she kissed me on the cheek. Laughing, I lost my balance and fell backward, knocking over the coffee tray sitting next to the couch. How embarrassing! Jan stretched out his hand and pulled me up. His hands were so strong. I knew at that very moment that I wanted to be with this man forever. He played tennis, was going to be a dentist, LOVED dogs, and had the kindest eyes. What more could a girl want?

Meeting Jan's mother… no… any mother, was difficult for me. I never knew how to respond when the inevitable questions about family came up. It made the most sense to just say, "They are no longer with us." That covered it. No one wanted to ask any more questions after that bit of information was nonchalantly stated. Sure enough, after the first hellos to Jan's mother in broken English, she smiled, showing her two top front teeth missing, and asked, "You mother here? Jan say you Polish? Notski?"

I didn't know it then, but for the rest of my life, the questions about origin and parents would be like the pointy, prickly "tag along" burrs stuck deep in between the pads of a dog's paw. You get pricked, feel the pain, get rid of the burr, and eventually, unexpectedly, step on another. I smiled and avoided answering by diverting his mom's attention to the kitchen. "What smells so good? Jan said Perogies."

"Yah, yah. Perogies? You know perogies?" Jan's mom, Marie, pointed to the pan on the stove with doughy blobs bobbing up and down in a grease splattered vat of searingly hot oil. As I stared at the sizzling perogies before me, it struck me how quickly the pale white dough turned a golden brown.

"I don't know perogies. What is inside?"

"Vegebles, park, and cheese."

Jan quickly clarified, "Mom, it's vegetables and pork." I could tell he was slightly uncomfortable and a bit annoyed.

"Oh! Don't worry, Ms. Marie. People tell me they can't understand me all the time. In fact, my professor called me into the office and told me to continue participating in the speech pathology program, I have to start "accent reduction" next semester. I feel your pain. Your English is fine."

Jan proceeded to repeat all I said – and probably more – in Polish for his mom. She looked up with her very rosy cheeks and rounded face and smiled. Then he said, "Seriously? That sucks for you. One of the Scottish guys in my class had to do the same thing. You really couldn't understand him most of the time. But I get you pretty well."

Marie motioned for me to try the perogy.

"Yummy! I didn't know what to expect, but this is good. Bet it's chock full of calories!"

Marie gave me a sincerely triumphant smile of appreciation. I could tell she was very proud of her cooking and Polish heritage. There were all things Poland in the house. The China cabinet was filled with brightly painted plates and cups boasting huge mountain scenes of snow. Several sets of brightly colored blue, red, and yellow wooden nesting dolls with splashes of white daisies surrounding the dolls' faces lined the shelving in the room. Intricate, lacey white doolies covered *every* surface in the house. It was also hard not to notice that all the furniture was covered with thick plastic.

At that site, a shiver went through me. The plastic-covered furniture lived in my childhood house as well. It reminded me of a time when I stole cookies and unlocked my brother's bedroom door because she didn't let him have breakfast or dinner the day before. *She* caught me and chased me through the house until I landed on the couch. While the fury of her punches pummeled my shoulders and side, I buried my face and tried to make my body invisible. The ultimate degradation occurred as I felt warm urine flow through my pajamas and the plastic stick to my skin, still helplessly defending myself, crouched on the couch. Funny, how the mind works. I pushed the thought away as I always did when I recalled unpleasantries. Such thoughts always made me question if my memory was playing tricks, but deep in my gut I knew my memories were correct.

"Isabella, my mom wants to know if you want more perogies? A drink maybe? We have water, tea, coffee and some juices, I think."

Brought out of my head space, I stammered, "Any Diet Coke?"

"What? Cake?"

"No, Coke, Diet Coke."

"What do you want?"

"C-o-k-e."

Jan laughed, "Maybe you do need that accent reduction. But, sorry, no soda allowed in this house."

"Actually, I'm fine. Are you ready to go to the courts? I can change there. I brought all my gear."

"Sure, let's get out here."

Jan spoke to his mom a bit and returned to me sitting on the plastic-covered floral couch. He had a big smile. Amazingly, with the exception of a few crooked bottom teeth, his teeth were all intact.

"Okay, ready."

Getting into his yellow VW bug, Jan looked so handsome to me.

"So, after we hit a bit, how about meeting my friends at the UPub. I think you already met one of them. His name is Ryk from the radio station. I ran into him right after you went to the university radio station a few weeks ago. HE told me you were cute. He didn't tell me how pretty you were. Those eyes."

I blushed and settled in. Huh, he knew Ryk. Interesting.

"Sure, I am game. I have the entire day off and that never happens. You might change your mind after you see my serve."

"Don't be ridiculous. I have checked you out a few times on the court. You have an athlete inside there. I'm sure of it."

Chapter 5

The rest of the year moved by quickly. Already upon me was the first semester of Sophomore year. I felt insanely grateful for Jan and his Dad! Over the course of the Spring and Summer, he put on new tires, changed the alternator, put in a new battery and water pump, fixed the clutch, and replaced the gear shifter – all for free. While I had a hard time accepting his generosity, I also knew he was a Polish angel sent at the right time. Jan and I were getting along well, and I was crazy about him. He could do no wrong in my eyes. He accepted me for me and didn't pry when I told him I didn't want to discuss my family. He wasn't nosy and got the hints that there was no need to have that conversation.

It was hard to believe that Christmas was a few weeks away, along with semester finals. This year was going to be different. I might actually be invited to a real family dinner. That was a hope I didn't want to jinx. I was cautiously optimistic with a wait-and-see attitude.

In between working and studying, I managed to see Jan almost every other day. He was kind and generous. He made me laugh at myself and never judged me. I was always welcome to come and stay at his place downtown that he shared with a roommate. My eyes were opened while I was there. He wasn't perfect. He and his roommate got high regularly. I wondered how the two of them were so successful in dental school. But I forgave him and even ignored the extent to which his roommate influenced him because I had never felt loved until him. I never had anyone who cared or told me I did a nice job.

I won gymnastic medals, softball and netball trophies, sailing trophies, and got all "A"s, but none of that was ever good enough. My accomplishments were expected, and God help me if I didn't meet those expectations. I was the baby in the family, and I knew the drill of terror if I didn't measure up. Jan recognized I was good at things. Good at school. Good at sports. Good at being responsible. He commented a few times that I was way too young to be carrying such heavy burdens at this point in life. I appreciated that. His recognition that I was a strong woman meant everything. I knew that I just did what any person would do in my situation – pull up the bootstraps and get the job done. I had to keep moving forward as I would be nothing without a degree.

I had improved in tennis a bit and finished my freshman season with a win. The UPub and radio station were fast becoming my home away from home. I was lucky to have met a group of people with whom I meshed well. There was Annie, aka "Beaner", Jenny, and Morgan to round out the female component of the "Sensational Seven", as we deemed ourselves. By now, Jan, Howard, Ryk, and I rounded out the Sensational Seven.

Not everything ran smoothly at the beginning of my Sophomore Fall semester. There was a brief moment of awkwardness that almost derailed me and the Sensational Seven. I enjoyed having conversations with Ryk during the four hours he sat for his dialysis and learned the procedural steps of home dialysis. I sat with him through dialysis any time possible. In November, just after my brother's birthday, suddenly Ryk attempted to kiss me when I was leaning over his shoulder, clearing one of his many tube lines. The kiss was so unexpected.

Ryk confused my willingness to sit with him at home

dialysis with love. I recall how I stood motionless until I gathered my thoughts. When asked what he was thinking, he was direct and to the point. He wanted to experience love, a wife, and family before it was too late. It was his fifth year on the kidney donor list, and with his rare blood type, the chances of receiving a kidney seemed further and further from his reach. I remember his exact words, "I love you. I have since you walked into my radio station. I can be here for you always. Marry me."

Ryk knew the value of life. He was the leader of the Sensational Seven. He organized our travel to music festivals and concerts. He organized the group's intramural sports participation. He was always available to take me to work when my car was out of service. He regularly had his friends working in the cafeteria line supply me with much appreciated meals, never letting on he knew how desperate my financial situation really was. He was the glue that kept the popsicle sticks together of one's model dream home. But Ryk was also reckless with his life. Driving with him in his beloved late 80s Dodge Charger, Shelby GLHS, was as scary as it was legendary around campus. I always thought his muscle car was secretly his weapon of rage against his private war.

Ryk partied every chance he got. He didn't worry about money, as he lived with his mother and received disability checks. He used his money for pot, beer, gas, and music. I wasn't sure if he ever actually entered any classroom. He was taking only one class a semester while I was slaving over fifteen credits while working three jobs.

Ryk was a force to be reckoned with as our fearless group leader. The summer following freshman year, during an Ocean and Sun music festival on the Eastern Seaboard beach town, Ryk gave us all a scare. While it was one of many, it was one of the worst. Famous for ignoring the warnings of his body, a close call was imminent. He drank and drank at that festival. We all knew he needed to get to the Oceanside Dialysis Center, where he made the appointment, but he didn't heed any of our pleas. Despite our stop-the-drinking protests, words of encouragement, and insistence he go, his appointment time came and went. In our dance circle, Ryk collapsed. His lips were blue, and his skin was white like the skin of a person afflicted with albinism.

"Shit, Ryk! Call 911! What the fuck? Are you crazy? You are stoned and drunk! Do you WANT to die?" I heard myself screaming at him. I was furious. How dare he do that to us? To me? It was like he had a death wish. All of us sat vigil at the hospital's ICU, awaiting a miracle. Ryk made it through – that time. Another chance to live life. I missed work that evening and thought about how it could have been Ryk 's obituary I was writing that night when I finally hit my bed and passed out.

Concerns about Ryk 's summer drama and November kiss attempt evaporated as the days wore on. The first week of December, after Italian class, my professor came to me and asked if my brother was going to be turning in his paper soon. Taken off guard, I stammered a bit, "My brother? I don't have a brother here."

But my professor was adamant. "Notski is your last name, no?"

"Yes, Notski is my last name."

"Well, I just figured my other student who is a Notski must be your brother. He's a sophomore, too."

"Oh, what's his first name?"

"Danny."

"Oh, I don't know him."

This exchange haunted me through the rest of the week. I

knew my last name was rare. I have never met another person with the same last name. The thought of having another Notski in the same year taking the same course was intriguing. Very curious. Who knew? Maybe I should reach out to this other Notski. I told the trusted Sensational Seven. Ryk threw in an impromptu shout-out on his radio show for the mysterious other Notski to no avail. If there was another named Notski, it seemed I may never meet him.

It was only three days before Christmas break. I decided to sit upstairs in the cafeteria as downstairs was pretty empty and quiet. Most were either last-minute cramming for exams or leaving for winter break. I was hungry and had $1.50. Enough for chocolate milk and a Snicker's.

While studying, Jenny came running over to me. "I think I found mystery Notski!"

"What? You are kidding? Where? Did you speak to him?"

"Yes! I was coming out of the Italian exam and heard a group of kids studying. Someone was giving 'Notski' a hard time about pronunciation. I thought it was going to be you when I turned the corner. When I didn't see you, I stood there and just said, 'Notski. Is there a Notski here?' A guy said yes!"

The look on my face said it all. The mystery man was found. The bigger question still loomed in the air – who was this Notski man, and were we related?

"You have to wait another hour. I told him I would find you and we would meet him at the UPub." Jenny was bubbling with excitement. She loved mystery and drama! She was so lovely. Petite with a perfect body, long, shiny brown hair , and a smile that was a perfect body, and a smile that was testament that her soul was pure. Every guy wanted to go out with Jenny, so that the mystery Notski would agree to meet her.

"Oh… MY… GOD! No fucking way! Fair Dinkum?"

"Yes, yes! In one hour, we are going to meet the mystery Notski. It's so exciting! I called reinforcements! Beaner and Howard are supposed to meet us. Morgan is already on her way home. Where's Jan? Let me guess – getting high before class with his roommate?"

"Ha, ha. He does not get high every day. But, no, he's not available today. You should know he's the first kid in the family becoming a doctor. He has a lot of pressure to succeed, you know?"

"Okay, but I don't get it. You don't drink, get high, or smoke, and yet you cut him so much slack!"

"Let's get back to mystery Notski please! What did he look like? Did he say he knew about me?"

"All I learned was that he didn't study much and was cramming till last minute so he couldn't talk. He is taller than you, has blonde hair and blue eyes. Don't get too excited, he's not exactly in shape."

An hour seemed like an eternity. I was finally going to meet the mystery Notski. Sitting at our usual UPub corner booth, we discussed all the insane possibilities.

"You don't know your grandparents, right?" Jenny asked.

"And you don't have any other relatives that you know of except your sister and brother?" Beaner chimed in. "Maybe he is from a secret out of wedlock tryst."

I was getting nervous. Howard already got a pitcher of beer for the celebratory meeting. I didn't drink beer. Never was one for a tinny. Diet Coke and tea. I don't know if I was still on auto pilot hearing "only blue-collar losers ever drink" from the subconscious childhood tape that ran regularly or if I really just didn't like the taste of beer. I tried it – twice. I didn't get the appeal. I was happy being the straight-laced jock drinking my Diet Coke. The clock was getting ready to strike twelve, and I was either going to turn into a pumpkin or meet a relative – maybe.

"Hey, maybe this guy is from another country too. Maybe he doesn't know about you either. This is so exciting."

"Alley oop! Look who just walked in. Is that him, Jen?" Beaner asked excitedly.

Jenny's smile broadened, and she jumped out of her seat to wave the mystery Notski over to our table. He was definitely taller than me by at least a foot. His hair was a dirty blonde, and his round face was a bit plump. He wore a wrinkled white preppy shirt and tan khakis. His Sperry shoes screamed preppy – a disheveled one – but still preppy. The kind of preppy that told you he came from money but didn't care one way or the other. His gut told me sports weren't his first priority. He smiled shyly and slowly raised his hand with one of those "hi" waves from the hip. I noticed he had huge feet as he approached.

"Hey. I am Danny. So, which of you is the other Notski?"

"She is!" My friends pointed in unison, as if the Sensational Seven members had rehearsed this very moment many times over.

"G'day. I'm Isabella. Come sit with us. Do you drink? Of course, you do." I managed to say with a little timid laughter.

Everyone sat very quietly and waited while the pitcher was passed around and glasses were filled. My stomach was churning, and I wasn't quite sure what to say. Is *this* person related to me? If he is, I don't know how. Danny chugged down his first beer, slammed down the glass, and bellowed out, "Cheers to the Notskis." What? Is this guy for real?

Howard jump-started the conversation. "Okay, inquiring

minds want to know, bro. What is your story? Are you related to

We all watched Danny as he stared at me for a few seconds and then looked at my friends. "I have no fucking idea."

Oh, a drinker and a potty mouth. This guy definitely couldn't be related. If he was, he had aliens for parents because his parents couldn't possibly be related to mine. Cussing and drinking gave that away.

"Well. Have you ever been to Australia?" Jenny asked.

"Nope. But I have been to New Zealand. Does that count?" Danny replied, laughing.

"Okay, okay. What about France?" Jenny persevered with about six other questions, to which Danny replied with all negatives.

Howard leaned into the group and said, "Hey, clearly you don't have an accent, but you guys look a little bit alike to me. What are your parent's names?"

Looking a bit uncomfortable squirming in the booth seat, he quickly provided us all with his parents' names. "Teddy and Susie. What about yours?"

Dread came over me. Seriously, I didn't think about having to actually ever say *their* names since I was twelve. In fact, I don't think I have said their names since the day I stayed with Mom and Dad "D" and left Australia. I mustered up verbalizing their names. Breathing felt like someone just stuffed a ball of cotton down my throat, and I had to choke it out.

"Phil and Francis. Ring any bells?"

At that moment, Danny's face changed. Turning pale, his eyes dropped down to the table, and he muttered, "Oh my fucking God!"

"What? Whaaaaat?" Jenny persisted. Howard and Beaner were on the edge of their seats. Precisely at that moment, Ryk came strolling over to the booth. "What is whaaaaat? What are we talking about?"

"Shhhhh, Danny Notski here is going to tell us. Right, Notski? I mean the Danny one," Jenny exclaimed.

Danny sat there, looking even more uncomfortable now. I could feel my chest beating and wondered if everyone else could hear my heart beat also.

All eyes were on Danny. He straightened up, motioned for Ryk to move out of the bench seat. I was on edge, thinking he was going to leave without telling us! Out of the booth, he motioned for me to stand up and took my hand. Without warning, he pulled me into his sweaty body, giving me a bear hug and blurting, "Hey, cuz! You are my cousin!"

I stared at him long and hard. My mind was reeling. How was this possible? Not only was he declaring himself as my cousin, but a first cousin! This cannot be! My parents never mentioned I had a cousin. As far as I knew, my grandparents on my father's side died long before I was born and talking about my mother's family was either a non-topic or taboo. Never knew which, and I never dared to ask. I only briefly heard about an aunt on my mother's side when I was nine after my father had a debilitating accident. Having a first cousin wasn't totally impossible. It could be plausible, as we didn't exactly have family gatherings like a Norman Rockwell poster.

"Well, aren't you going to say anything, cuz? This is awesome. I've got an Aussie cuz!" Danny hugged me again.

"What? Um, ah, um, are you SURE?"

"Yes! My father is your father's brother! I remember meeting your Dad twice when I was a kid. He was skinnier than my Dad and soft spoken. I think your dad had some kind of surgery. My Dad's a heart surgeon, and I guess your mom called him. That's all I remember. I don't think a lot of love was between the two of them though because my mother told me she hated your mother and vice versa."

This information was all too much. I was overwhelmed. Falling back into my seat, I felt numb from head to toe. There was only one thing to do. I still had one final left. Get up, go to work, and study tonight. I needed an "A" on my final. I couldn't fall apart now. I didn't even know if this guy was for real. I didn't know how I was going to find out if he was crackers or not. I couldn't, I wouldn't, ask the only people who would know.

Punching me in the shoulder, Beaner was elated. "You have a cousin! No shit!"

The punch woke me up. "This is too much. I gotta go." I collected my rucksack and clumsily threw on my coat, scarf, and hat. I suddenly felt nauseous. I didn't expect *this*. I didn't know what to do with this information. Bugger me! I had a first cousin? This shit was getting too real.

"Hey, cuz. Don't bolt yet. Here's my number. It's a shocker for me, too! Can't wait to swap stories. I'm sure you got doozies to tell!"

I grabbed the white-lined paper now with grease from chicken wings and stuffed it in my coat pocket. I was going to need a minute. A long minute.

Chapter 6

Waiting for the downpour to end, standing outside the back entrance of the newspaper, I reflected upon the past months. Since learning of my cousin, Danny, I wasn't too sure if it was a blessing or a curse. It was also hard to believe I was nearing the end of my third academic year. Jan and I were still doing well despite some brief breakups. Unfortunately, my beloved cat, Suki, was dealt a bad hand and had not been doing well the past weeks.

When Jenny found Suki under a campus dumpster in my freshman year, I gave the silver-grey, long-haired cutie a home. She needed bottle feeding. Suki had a prolapsed intestine. Her prognosis was poor, and she was going to have to be a fighter to make it to the age of three or four. I knew she needed a name befitting her fearless determination to survive in a dumpster, alone and motherless. I thought of the Japanese World gymnastics Champion of the seventies, Tsukahara, and how a simple half-twist onto the vault changed the course of gymnastics. Tsukahara felt right, and I hoped a miracle could magically change her fate. Shortened to Suki, the little fur ball never failed to curl in my armpit and purr us both to sleep. I knew I wouldn't have her forever, so every day with her was a good one.

The past year I decided to move in with Jan. My brain was more mature than most, but sexuality still felt unknowingly foreign. For months, Jan patiently dealt with a girlfriend who did not orgasm. No matter how he tried, my mind would never allow my body to feel good. Invariably, I would pull Jan up from his soft kisses between my thighs and make it all about him. Jan seemed satisfied but not always happy. I, however, always felt as if I diverted the unholiest of sins that would surely send me straight to hell. I didn't know how to, and I definitely did not know how to allow someone to love me in the physical sense. Eventually, I succumbed. Jan became the master of my first orgasm.

The night my flower blossomed, it was surely unexpected. Now that Jan was living without a roommate, sexual freedom was a welcome benefit. Jan had just been accepted into the cranial facial surgical program internship and was ecstatic. I was just accepted to the United States gymnastics senior gymnastics coaching camp under the tutelage of former Olympian, Brent Lindi. We had a lot to celebrate.

Jan lit a ring of vanilla and lavender-scented candles. The glow on the walls of the historic building apartment seduced us into a lull of calmness. We feasted upon steak and broccoli and wine spritzers. He finished off the dinner with a poppy seed roll his mother made the day before. We ate. We laughed. He got high – I still refused the herb. Everything could not have been more perfect. After dinner, he leaned over the table and gave the type of gentle kiss that said, "I am here with you." He touched my cheek and brushed away strands of my long hair. His eyes were twinkling, and his smile radiated the room. He slowly ran his fingers through my long hair. I tilted back my neck while he slipped each sleeve off my shoulders. I could not take my eyes off of him. The sexual tension was thick. I ached for his tongue to devour all of me. He softly whispered, "This is okay. Let go, Isabella. Get out of your head."

Jan keenly sensed he had me unwound and dedicated himself to me until the release of joy and tears intertwined. I allowed my body to experience the sweet, glorious explosion. That single moment felt like a weight was lifted. It changed me a bit. I found I was a bit kinder to work colleagues and to friends. I laughed more. The power of *feeling* was exhilarating. I would replay that night in my mind many times over that year. No matter how I tried, however, I always felt oddly uneasy about feeling good. It was as if I was on high alert for an unseen monster to steal away my happiness at any moment. Life taught me early on that happiness was followed by vicious, hurtful blows.

The year came and went. I learned my cousin had a better childhood than I but not a fairy tale. While he didn't physically suffer abuse, an element of emotional abuse was evident. Clearly, dysfunction ran in the gene pool. After our first meeting, we tried to study together. It was clear university participation was expected. He was to follow in his father's – my uncle's – medical footsteps. I knew he didn't have it in him.

Danny's mother had a home near the university, and he was living there alone. Danny's parents were divorced when he was in middle school, and he was shuffled from parent to parent. Danny didn't strike me as very resilient. During the sophomore Spring semester, Danny's mother and boyfriend let Danny know he was no longer welcome. With that news, I volunteered my apartment as a refuge. He didn't have to worry about money as he had plenty of that supplied by his father. He occasionally worked with one of his friends at a gas station, but mainly he partied, went West for downhill skiing, and raced motor cross.

While I thought it would be great to have a cousin living with me, I could not have been more wrong. Danny had no boundaries, nor did he respect the boundaries of others. He ate any and all food in the fridge without replacing it. He brought his friends without warning. He brought his girlfriends without warning, and modesty was non-existent. He never cleaned up after himself or his guests. The aforementioned, combined with two traumatized young people from dysfunction devoid of the ability to communicate, was disastrous. After Cuz moved out, we failed to stay in touch. Ce la vie. I didn't have the strength to carry Danny's burden, and I sensed he was not willing to change his laissez-faire ways.

Life went on, and so did my crazy schedule of school and work. Back to the daily grind of the newspaper, my shift seemed never-ending. Finally, the rain stopped. It was eleven-thirty p.m., and my midnight shift at the eye bank was next. A quick wave to the Sunpaper security officer in the back parking lot, and I dashed through the puddles to the underpass. It was the closest and cheapest place to park. As I stepped off the curb and proceeded under the turnpike overpass, a chill went up my spine. My inner voice made hair stand up on my arms. My instinct said to turn around. I shook it off. No biggie. I have been parking here for almost two years and never had trouble. While there were only dim lights at the north and south end of the lot, it was enough light to see one younger man getting into his car to my left and another leaning against his car just a few down from mine.

My inner voice nagged at me to turn around and ask someone to walk me to my car. I told myself I was being ridiculous. I was just exhausted and overworked. I shrugged it off, thinking it was simply anxiety. Checking for my keys, I firmly placed them in my hand in a ready position. As I approached my car, the man leaning against his door got in his Toyota. "There," I thought, "nothing to worry about." Relieved, my whole body sighed. Slipping the key in the lock, I heard the

Toyota's engine nearing me. My door still open, I started to take off my coat to throw it into the back seat. Suddenly, Toyota man jumped out of his car and grabbed me by the hair, throwing me off balance. I tripped and fell to the concrete.

The assault happened so quickly. The man's smell was overbearing. It was clear he had not showered for days. Terror engulfed my body and mind. As he grabbed my arms, I responded with powerful screams and flailing legs in attempts to get away. The noxious smell of his putrid breadth traveled through me as he grabbed at my blouse and ripped the buttons, exposing my chest.

I felt the vibration of a car on the overpass above. I tried to scream again, but my voice failed me. I continued to kick when the grotesque creature's grip loosened as he unzipped his pants. At that very moment, a car came into the underpass parking lot. I was saved. The rest was a blur.

"Mam, are you okay?" It was the security officer, Ito, whom I waved goodbye to as I left the newspaper back parking lot only a few minutes ago. I lay there. I couldn't move, speak, or cry. The security guard informed me, "The police are on their way."

The police came and took my report. Dazed, I heard myself talking but didn't recognize my own voice. It was as if I left my body and I was watching someone else attending to the tasks at hand. I felt so stupid. How could I have been so careless? Why didn't I listen to my gut? Why didn't I know what kind of Toyota he was driving? Why didn't I carry mace? Why didn't I fight harder? So many 'why's'. No answers.

I coped by telling myself that I was only assaulted but not raped, so it wasn't that bad. My childhood taught me how to compartmentalize and reject pain and fear, and my abilities did not disappoint in this situation. I focused on the positive. The management at the Sunpaper provided me with a space inside the gated, well-lit parking lot when I worked evening shifts. Jan was more attentive and overprotective. I began to feel suffocated and had no idea what to do in my current reality. I buried the pain of the experience – it would not get the better of me.

During that Junior year, Spring came, and with it came the university's annual intramural sports competition. The Sensational Seven signed up for co-ed softball. Truth be told, most of the sensational seven looked forward to the carefree campus party vibe more than the sports participation. Gathering for our first practice, Howard declared himself as coach. He made it no secret that his only goal was to win. "Okay, let's see how everyone fields the ball." Howard scrutinized each of our skills batting balls. A half hour went by, and he called us in for position assignments. Beaner was going to pitch, Jenny left field, Morgan at first base, and I at third base. The guys were to fill in the remaining positions, and Howard had willing friends if needed. It was decided that we would practice once a week, and those who could would also practice on Saturday mornings.

Practice started the first week of April, and we had to be ready by May 18. The date will be forever seared in my brain. Ryk organized a trip to watch the May 16 Preakness horse race at Pimlico Racetrack. I did not commit as I knew it would cost money I didn't have. Everyone was giddy with excitement about the Preakness during our last softball practice. Despite getting the day off and getting $20 from Ryk, I couldn't go. Suki had had a grand mal seizure the morning of Preakness, so I raced her to the vet. She was paralyzed from the waist down and had severely labored breathing. I knew the vet was right – I would have to put Suki down. She deserved a quiet, peaceful passing, no matter how much it pained me. I left the vet clinic despondent. In my car, I tuned in the radio dial. The local news was on. There was an accident outside the Pimlico grounds. I didn't have to find out anymore – I just *knew*.

The next weeks were filled with funerals and sorrow. Jenny and Ryk had lost their lives. Beaner was fighting for hers. The sadness of loss was surreal and unyielding. They were my family. It was decided that no services would be held until Beaner improved. She had a punctured lung, shattered fibula in one leg, and fractured tibia in the other. Her nickname was Beaner because of her precision throws on the basketball court. Her future was uncertain. Miraculously, Beaner spent only two days in ICU and was home a week later.

Those gathered at the burial site were stoic with faces dripping with tears. Ryk no longer had to wait for a kidney. Mourners from the university and the radio station paid homage to his spirit. I felt enormously guilty, and every swallow was difficult. My first thought after the tragedy was, "it could have been me." I felt selfish. The loss was confounding. Ryk recently shared he was engaged to his dialysis nurse. Seeing her young face deflated without hope was too much to bear. I stood on the sidelines with Howard, Beaner, and Jan. I felt ashamed and could not face Ryk's family or fiancé. The last prayers were said. Ryk's four favorite albums were placed on top of the coffin under a flower arrangement that was designed in the shape of a musical note. The hydraulics lowered the casket.

I watched the impression my foot left on the freshly sprung grass with each step I took walking across the graveyard lawn back to the car. Jan had to go back to the dental clinic. After hugging Jan goodbye, I filled my mind with finishing the day's tasks to avoid pain. "Isabella, please wait." It was Ryk's mother.

I slowly turned to see a woman I didn't recognize. Despite countless days spent with Ryk during dialysis, I wasn't positive this woman *was* his mother. She was a shell of the self I had come to know. Her voice wavered and crackled as she tried to speak. "Isabella, I would like you to come to the house with us."

"I don't know if I have time. I have to get to work."

"Please, Isabella, there is something I need to give you."

What could I say but, "Of course." On the way to Ryk's house, I could not imagine what she had to give me. Pulling up to the familiar driveway, Ryk's beloved Shelby was parked off to the side. I sighed with relief when I saw Howard helping Beaner out of the car and into her wheelchair. I walked over to join them. We didn't speak. There was nothing to say.

Mourners came in and milled around as if they were lost in a library. No one spoke, and the air felt heavy inside the living room. Ryk's dialysis chair was still occupying the righthand corner of the den. Running my index finger over the brown leather, I realized Ryk's mother had entered the room. "Isabella, thank you for coming. I have something for you. It's in Ryk's bedroom." I silently followed her to his bedroom as if in a trance. There, she handed me an envelope prepared by Ryk. Clearly, he had prepared his exit as he wrote with a "knowing" that he would not live to see a kidney transplant.

Trembling, I opened the thick, cream-colored envelope. Multicolored tiny hearts arranged in a larger heart adorned the card's front. Inside, the crisply formed cursive message was simple: *I love you. I have always loved you. In case…here are the keys to my car and a check for next semester. Yours, Ryk*

His beloved Shelby and tuition payment. I couldn't take either. It wouldn't be right. He had a fiancé. I was not her. I handed back the cream envelope. I looked at his mom and handed it back.

"I can't." Walking out of Ryk's house, I felt alone. Only gravity kept me moving forward.

Chapter 7

Another week to push through and another funeral. Standing over Jenny's small body lying in the casket, it was hard to imagine just days before we were practicing for intramural sports. She looked so serene, like a perfect doll dressed for a proper English tea party. I thought she would have loved the white floral shirt dress her mother chose. Jenny always had a keen sense of style. It's a funny world. Focusing on what the dead were wearing in the casket. As if this mattered at all.

When I saw Jenny's mom, despite digging deep, I could only come up with a mumbled attempt of, "So sorry." No one *really* knows what to say to another who just lost a loved one. And when it is a child dying before the parents, logic and reason become unraveled. The *celebration of life* tactic seemed daft under the tragic circumstances. Jenny's life was cut short. No matter how you try to soften the language, loss is loss. The living move on, but Jenny's family would never be whole again. Using cliches and fluff was not going to eek away at the dense rind encircling such deep loss.

"Jenny was a vibrant, young woman headed for a career in the world of economics," the priest continued. "God is love. Life is not only what we see, hear, or touch. Life is a puzzle. Each piece bound by edges that continue to reveal how we live. Jenny lived a good life. We must believe that today the emptiness we feel is not empty at all. If we allow God to lead us, we will find the empty space is full of love and not empty at all. Our human form is a gift from God. He will guide us and fill our hearts with memories and love. Jenny has passed, but we will keep her in our hearts and minds."

Listening to the priest's proclamation that life was filled with perfect spaces reached my ears like screech marks of chalk on a chalkboard. Life may never fill our empty spaces. That day, the space was a sinkhole that swallowed Jenny. I wondered if the goodness of Jenny was too much weight for this world to hold. I was determined to remember Jenny. Her snorting laughter that made all of us laugh more. The way her wardrobe always matched perfectly, each outfit punctuated with a special hat or pop of color adorning her shoes and boots. Jenny could convince you with her sweet voice and pearly white smile that having a root canal would be fun. She never missed giving a birthday card to any of us. She packed snacks in cute wicker lunch baskets lined with red-and-white-checked satin. Jenny made everyone she met feel like their lives mattered.

It seemed as if it was a time warp as my mind reeled through moments with Jenny. Returning from Christmas break, while at lunch, Jenny exclaimed she got engaged on Christmas day! All of us were quite surprised as she only dated Paul for three months. Jenny was easy to fall in love with. She always had men asking her out. She was petite but strong. She was agreeable but firm. She was intelligent and witty. I realized how easy it must have been for Paul to have fallen in love with her. Jenny assured all of us that he was the one. She seemed so confident and happy, so we were happy for her. When Jenny's father came to the podium to speak, thoughts drifted back to how she and I first met.

I did not yet have a car. The bus was my only option. It was windy and pouring rain, and I was nearly soaked walking from the bus stop to the student center. The wind had turned Jenny's umbrella inside out. She was laughing at herself as she failed to get the umbrella back into working order. I asked if I could help. She replied in typical sunny Jenny fashion, "Sure, if we don't fly away like Mary Poppins first!" The umbrella's flimsy connecting rods broke, and there was no fixing it. Jenny made light of it and laughed and got wet.

We drank hot tea and shared a bit about ourselves drying off in the student center. She loved life. It was so obvious. She was an only child. She was easy to talk to and embraced new cultures. She had inquiries about all aspects of Australian culture. She shared how she was adopted from Japan and was glad her parents were second-generation Japanese. We talked and talked. We bonded over our love for animals. She had a Maltese. I told her about my beloved Australian Shepherd mix. When she learned I didn't have a car, she had no hesitation. "Then, I will be your from now on! Not a problem at all!" I knew right then we would be friends. I was right. Jenny was an angel with whom I was lucky enough to have had for a brief moment of time in my life.

Depression wasn't a word I would have ever used to describe myself in college. I equated being depressed with being weak. I was a survivor. Survivors weren't weak. I emerged from the Spring tragedy determined that I would meet my goals and enjoy my life. Entering my last year of university felt awkward and surreal. Despite the past year, I was determined to make the most of my last year. I was optimistically hopeful. I continued working with Brente Lindi and passed the USA Gymnastics judging test series. My sights were set on finishing college and getting a coaching spot on a national gymnastics team. I had passed several coaching exams over the summer and received interest from several national gymnastic training centers. Medicine and speech pathology were not even making the list.

Daily life moved forward. Besides having to inform funeral directors when writing obituaries that the greeting, "We skin 'em, you print 'em," wasn't the most appropriate anymore; overall, life seemed good – maybe even great. It had been three months since Beaner left the hospital. Beaner was healing nicely, and Morgan and I took turns shuttling her from place to place. Beaner convinced me to let her drive with her soft cast on. Only once she failed to push the brake quickly enough when approaching a red light. The Ghia barely touched the bumper of another car – it was more of a soft bumper-to-bumper kiss. The other driver jumped out of his car with such swiftness it was hard not to feel like we were watching an action movie. He was not happy. Beaner also got out of the car. The man stood, open-mouthed and flabbergasted! Staring at Beaner calmly standing on her leg that donned the black metal robotic-looking mechanism evoked a high-pitched yell.

"What are you doing? You shouldn't be driving with that, that, thing!" Spit on the left side of his mouth combined with his flailing arms was nothing short of theatrical as he pointed to Beaner's leg. His face looked as if it would burst any moment like the Wilkie Wonka girl that turns purple and pops from eating the taboo blueberry candies. Luckily, Beaner, with her quick thinking, calmed the man.

"I'm so sorry. Typically, I would agree but, I lost my best friend when a drunk driver slammed into us, and we are going to the funeral."

"Yes," I chimed in. I spat on my finger, wiped the man's bumper scuff, and said, "See, a little spit and all is good. We really need to go. Should we exchange insurances?"

The man looked stunned. Begrudgingly, the man turned around and went back to his car and left. Beaner and I looked at each other. It was hard to believe she came up with that! The stress of losing a friend manifested itself in odd ways. I looked at Beaner and tried to get out the words, "I'm driving." Now positions switched; it only took one look, and we cracked up. It was as if a telepathic connection between Beaner and I formed at that very second. The release of laughter was welcomed – even if it was a short burst of relief. Driving to the university, I decided it was time to share what happened at Ryk's after his funeral. I told Beaner about the conversation I had with Ryk's mom. Beaner looked at me with one of those expressions saying "what the…" I responded quickly.

"Crikey, who would have expected that? I felt like a sheared sheep!" I declared.

Beaner started laughing again. "A sheared sheep! What does that even mean?"

"You know – naked, awkward, caught with my pants down." I managed to reply between laughter.

"Got it now! I know – my crazy driving with a cast is exactly what Ryk would have done, Isabella! You know, in all sincerity, I believe he was in love with you. His engagement to the dialysis nurse was out of desperation. I believe he knew he had limited time and wanted to make the most of it."

"I know, but I could have never seen myself with Ryk. He knew I was with Jan. Besides, there was never any physical attraction, and I am too young for marriage. It felt so wrong when I read the card. What if his fiancé would have seen that?"

"Ryk was Ryk. He wanted to live sixty years in one year. You know that!"

"You're right. He was definitely reckless with his life. When I think about all the concerts we had to leave because Ryk drank too many beers. He never followed the doctor's protocol – never!

The number of times we were pulled over and Ryk convinced the cop to escort us to the ER!"

Beaner chuckled. "Ryk was quite the charmer with that big, impish smile. Oh God, remember when we were driving to a Bowie concert, and Ryk hit something in the middle of the road! We got out and a poor fox's paw was hanging from the wheel well!"

The thought of that night. The thought of Ryk's Shelby racing through the pitch-black hilly roads as if he were a world-class formula one racer forced a smile. "Well, here we are. The radio station and Upub will never be the same." Arriving at the campus with Beaner had its advantages, as her handicap permit was a bonus. Watching Beaner to get along on her crutches, my only thought was that Glenda the Good Witch needed to appear every day until graduation. I couldn't handle any more heartache.

Days and months went by relatively smoothly. I missed my friends, my cat, Suki, and having the closeness with Jan. I knew life would never be the same. Innocence was long gone, and there were no unique words of wisdom one could say to soothe the feeling of loss in my heart. Christmas break was closing in upon us. As the remaining members of the Sensational Seven, we decided to enter into the rugby Christmas tournament at the university. We were dedicating our participation to Ryk and Jenny. Howard agreed to coach, despite knowing little about rugby. Howard was very confident we would win, and we could dedicate the trophy to Ryk. Beaner volunteered to help with coaching after reading a rugby play manual, but playing was still impossible.

Rugby game day was upon us, and the morning greeted us all with a thoroughly muddy field from the nightly downpour. Despite the muddy conditions, it was a fair-like atmosphere on the field grounds. Food vendors lined the sidelines. Artisan tents offered wares from jewelry to carved wooden furniture. Commemorative t-shirts marking the charity event were passed out to each participant. Proceeds went to a local charity that provided toys and meals for those less fortunate. That seemed fitting as Ryk and Jenny were always empathetic toward others' misfortune and struggle. Even if we didn't win, we had the opportunity to reconnect with their spirit during the event. We had only one slight problem. Howard had no clue how to play rugby, and those we recruited were not exactly top-shelf athletes. Nonetheless, our team, named the "Jenryks", was determined to be *the* victor.

Howard tried to convince sixteen players – of which nine were female – that being muddy and playing the two forty-minute periods with a fifteen-minute break was sheer bliss. It wasn't the best "pitch" of a field, but then we were in America, playing on a football field. Tentatively, we practiced running phases of schlepping the ball forward. With each pass, we became muddier until all but one of us slipped and fell. Muddy but exhilarated, we were undeterred. "Knock-ons" were going to be frequent for sure! We could only hope we all remained healthy throughout the match as we had only one extra player on our team.

The kick-off result was not a good omen. Half the team reverted to American football and was constantly called out for numerous violations. Our dream of victory was more than questionable. We managed to get through the first forty minutes unscathed. It was 0–0. Howard delivered a sappy but motivational speech, and we were re-energized. The first few plays were uneventful in the second half, and then there was a scrum. A scrum in rugby is the equivalent to a group of screaming preteens pushing and piling on top of one another to get close to

Boys To Men. A scrum is messy, and those on the bottom are like the ingredients inside the sandwich smashed between the bread. I heard myself scream in pain. In a flash, I realized I had injured my left foot.

The medics were called to the field. Once on the stretcher, I knew it was not good. Howard couldn't believe the luck! "We are cursed! The only player who knows any of the rules is now out!"

Jan followed the ambulance in his VW bug to the hospital. Once there, the awkwardness of family reared its ugly head. Telling the medical staff that I had no parents or relatives to call begot both pity and confusion. I am sure they found the notion of "no relatives" incomprehensible as they repeatedly asked for closest of kin contact information. I kept repeating that I had no one to call. I only had Jan. Luckily, I turned eighteen the year before, and I could sign for my own surgery. One of the emergency room nurses took notice of my situation and asked if I had a boyfriend. I replied, "had" was the operative word as I didn't honestly know where Jan and I stood. Nonetheless, and probably out of pity, a nurse called Jan in the exam room. I did feel somewhat better as Jan may not have been an orthopedic resident, but he was a fourth-year dental student.

X-rays made it clear the injury was not a simple fracture. An orthopedic specialist came and explained that I would need extensive surgery due to the severity of the breaks. Growing up exposed to the medical field, I trusted science. I was prepped for surgery. Jan assured me that he would be there when I awoke. When I came to from surgery, Jan kept his promise. He had made it to the hospital and told me the orthopedic surgeon said all would be well with a little physical therapy and patience. Jan was quick to point out that patience was not my strong suit.

The cast width extended four inches longer on each side of

my foot. I had crushed my first and fifth metatarsal bones, which required several metal rings and thick straight pins on each side of my foot. Hence, the very wide cast and a new nickname – "Platypus". Beaner was thrilled that she single-handedly came up with my new nickname. I wasn't so sure if I liked it, but for the remainder of university, I was called either Platty or Platypus. It was a much better nickname than a few others – Chotski-Notski, Flopsie-Notski, and Dizzy Lizzy (based on my middle name Elizabeth).

Recovery would be long. My patience was short. Cast changes were required weekly. I drove a standard clutch. I didn't know how I would manage. The stars aligned, and Jan secured me an old automatic Dodge Charger parked idly behind his Dad's VW garage. Jan's Dad said I could use it while I was recovering so I could drive. While I was more than grateful for the use of the Dodge, I couldn't decide if the hood locks made me look cool or a complete wanker! Either way, just having wheels I could access with one bum leg was a miracle in itself!

Miracles are all around us – we just have to see them! That's what Mom and Dad "D" always said. My childhood best friend's mom was like a mom in many ways. Mom "D" knew that living in my home environment was nothing short of Carrie meets Chucky. The daily uncertainty of what waited behind the door was more stress than the actual beatings or verbal tirades. Mom "D" never directly spoke about my mother, but she let me know that *I* was worth something. Mom "D" came to watch her daughter every gymnastics meet, while my parents never came to one. Mom "D" truly believed that tomorrow would always be a better day just because it was another day. If ever there was a time I needed to adopt Mom "D"'s mantra, it was now.

After opening the medical bill, how I was going to pay the

hospital debt consumed my thoughts. It felt like an insurmountable weight. It would become an albatross around my neck over the next decade. There was a silver lining, which was that I became wiser as a result of my slight mishap on the rugby field. Valuable lessons were learned. Any job I would take after graduation must have healthcare insurance. I learned the best policy was to never play rugby with a group of American footballers who don't know the rules. Finally, I learned that no matter what the situation was, there was always an absurdity of comedy. I was now Pladdy, and that was that. Looking down at my cast, it was clear I was not going to be playing team tennis my last Spring season. Life's uncertainty demanded contingency plans, and I just didn't have one.

Chapter 8

Jan was a quiet, even-tempered man. He was intelligent, kind, and confident. Unfortunately, he was also physically absent for most of the time we were a couple. He was, however, very patient and caring while I was frustrated, navigating life with my platypus cast. Jan would say I lacked appreciation for the nuance of his juggling a doting mother and a girlfriend. If he wasn't at school, he was helping his mom. This was a notion with which I had no experience. I was not comfortable around people's parents. I never saw myself as a child. I also learned to deflect any conversation about family or heritage. I knew from experience that I was silently being judged when I gave the response that I had no family relationships. I had more than one friend tell me that their parents thought I was a troublemaker because I didn't have a relationship with my parents or family. In college psychology, I read in the text how children from dysfunction and abuse would become drug users, prostitutes, and criminals.

I didn't have a drug or alcohol problem. I had no eating disorders. I didn't come from a poor or underrepresented family background. I escaped a world of abuse and fear and had no rage. I worked tirelessly to support myself and make good grades. My only vices were Snickers bars, chocolate milk, and Diet Coke. I totally thought the psychology text got it all wrong. Loneliness, insecurity, and a lack of trust were not chapters discussed in the textbook. They should have been. I was not a textbook case. I lived life as it came. But by the end of my senior year, I feared I may begin to write a new chapter that included the challenges of feeling hollow.

Despite my friends and bosses perceiving me as a social butterfly, possessing a positive outlook and generous nature, they didn't realize that inside I often felt hollow. Even when I was around people, the isolation I felt inside sometimes felt like yoga leggings that were too tight! Necessary but suffocatingly uncomfortable. I never thought of myself as super smart or talented. I did think my older sister was incredibly smart. She met the criteria for membership in the Mensa Club. Even though I had never met anyone in the Mensa Club other than her, I was pretty sure resilience and common sense were more important. I was keen on common sense but still tended to follow my heart. Wherever that took me, in my mind's eye, was always good enough.

With my continued foot surgery rehabilitation, I was slowly nearing normalcy. Patience is said to be a virtue. Whoever came up with that ditty did not have a cast so wide that knitted caps became a bonified fashion statement for feet. I think I was the first student to suggest a knitted tuque could be cool outerwear and not just a cap! There was also the fun distraction of using the tested technique of scratching inside the cast with a yardstick. I tried to be patient and follow the doctor's orders. But the closer I got to a hundred percent, the harder it was to wait.

I was ready to dance and play tennis again, spot gymnasts and get back to living. In that spirit, I decided that a make-over was just what I needed. I had never worn my hair any way except long and straight. It was easy to manage. I lived in a ponytail because there was no other style for an athlete! I never had bangs, and I didn't believe in having to take more than fifteen minutes to get ready to go anywhere. That said, I decided in my Senior year of college it was time to become more mature and sophisticated.

I set out for my new look. I thought I would surprise Jan with a new and refreshed me. Morgan always had short hair, so my first obvious lead was to ask her for help in finding a stylist. She provided me with her stylist's name and number, and was confident I would successfully bedazzle Jan. The day of the hair appointment, I was not so confident, and my gut was telling me to cancel! Yup, that gut of mine was always there like a best friend. Again, I didn't listen. With great trepidation, I went to the address Morgan provided. It was in a stylish section of downtown Baltimore. I felt hopeful. When I arrived, the atmosphere was inviting and spa-like. Assuming that I was the typical age of a senior in college, the stylist offered me champagne. I had never had *champagne* prior to that day, and I found it to be quite tasty and refreshing. I also welcomed glass top-offs while browsing through numerous magazines of gorgeous women with short hair. I was ready to embrace a new me!

I sat down in the stylist's chair. My stylist approached me, "My, my, what a beauty we have here. I am Sasha. Oh, that was nice of Morgan to send you over." Sasha had quite the presence. He reminded me of the wedding planner character in Steve Martin's movie, Father of the Bride. He was tall and thin and extremely handsome. He had the flamboyant hand gestures when he spoke that said he most likely preferred men. Sasha looked at me for quite a while from every angle, and only the champagne kept me from feeling like a nervous wreck! His personality was effervescent and infectious. He smiled. I smiled. He looked quizzical; I looked quizzical. It felt like I was in an old silent black and white movie.

After the initial introduction and a few glasses of liquid courage, my champagne brain and I were now glued to the seat. Sasha cheerfully stated I had beautiful eyes, and the cut he was about to give would accentuate my baby blues. He promised I was going to love what I saw. I grabbed a champagne refill and crossed my fingers. As I sipped, he snipped. Sheer panic ensued! It began. He started the first cuts of eight inches all around. I watched my long brown locks get discarded like hair caught in the shower drain! Panic set in again when he began to chop another inch or so and taper my now shortened bob look. Sasha had a strict rule when a new do was a bit drastic – I was not allowed to see myself in the mirror. Sasha explained his method of mirror banning during the cut was a sure safeguard, so drama was kept to a minimum.

It felt like an eternity, and my anxiety level was only tempered by the champagne. Finally, the cut was done. Sasha was clearly proud of his masterpiece, "And now, my dear Isabella, the new and improved, sophisticated you! Are you ready?"

"I can't glue it back now, can I, matey? This is my brave face, but I am more nervous than I expected I would be!" My face turned white when he spun me around, and I saw the new do! Was that ME in the mirror? Staring at myself as he blow-dried and shaped, I said nothing. I was in shock! I just kept drinking. I didn't recognize myself. Looking away from the mirror, tears beginning to flow, the other stylists commented on how good the cut looked. My gut was right – I was not emotionally ready for such a transformation! I definitely knew it would take a while to get used to. The other thing I knew – it would grow back!

When I got back home for dinner, Jan was dumbfounded. "Why didn't you tell me, Isabella?" was his first reaction in the form of a question that came out in a stutter. Not exactly the reaction for which I was hoping! "Well, Jan, I didn't know I had to. Do you like it?"

"It will take some getting used to, but you are still beautiful no matter what hair cut you have." I guess having to please his mom and patients came in handy because Jan knew how to be diplomatic and play it safe. I knew the true test would be when I walked into work for the midnight shift at the eye bank. Then I could gauge exactly how drastic others viewed my transformation. Somehow, I got through dinner without breaking down in tears. I avoided looking in the mirror until I had to leave for work.

That night I headed to my eye bank job. The building was located next to the main downtown hospital. My job entailed either removing the cornea or the entire eye of a corpse, the quick transference for transport, and often a trip to the airport with the donated organ. I started the job in my sophomore year, thanks to Jan's connection. I didn't mind the midnight shift as it was typically quiet, and I could sit in the office and study. This night, however, was not a quiet one. A call came through for me to go to the city morgue and extract both eyes from a late twenty-something young man who was killed in a car accident. Timing was everything when organs are donated, so I jumped into the county vehicle, turned on the emergency lights, and sped to the morgue.

Once I entered the building at the morgue, I had to check in with a security guard at the front entrance. Joey was on duty. He was a kind man. He was married and had three children. He was an easygoing and unexpectedly always cheery man. That night when I walked in, he definitely did a double-take.

"Whoa! Isabella! Is that you? Oooh la la, you are looking good!"

"Aw Joey, you say that to all the girls!" I quickly replied. In reality, it made me smile and gave me a bit more confidence about my new look. Then again, I thought to myself that I was much younger than Joey, and he was a kind-hearted man. Perhaps he didn't like it as much as he said.

"No way, Isabella. I mean it. You look great! Too bad you are having a date with a dead young man instead of a live one!"

"Yeah, yeah. So, what's the story with the donor? You have his chart and orders, or is the info in the back?"

"I left it in the usual place. Poor dude. I guess I better let you get to it. Always good to see you."

Joey walked me down the long hallway. The hallway felt like an empty subway station in New York City, but I was no longer affected by the space. It was tiled with stark white subway tile and had a faint echo when Joey and I spoke. My first time going through the morgue was a bit scary. It got easier as time went on, but I was never totally at ease until I completed the task and returned the body back to the roll-out compartment. The final "click" of the metal drawer hardware always prompted an audible sigh of relief.

"Okay, Isabella. I will let you do your job. Buzz me if you have any problems." With that, Joey opened the stainless steel cabinet drawer. The body did not yet show signs of rigidity. Looking at the tag on the donor's right big toe was the name A. Brown. "Okay Joey, I appreciate it. I am sure Mr. Brown and I will get along just fine." Joey turned and left, and the door to the morgue slammed shut.

It always struck me that no matter what your position or circumstances were in life, the tag on the big toe was the last record anyone assigned you. Deep in thought, I started to prepare for the eye removal procedure. I had great respect for each eye donor and always said hello to them by name. I knew they would not answer, but I felt it was the respectful thing to do. I thought it was only human to honor the shell of the body and thank their spirit for being kind enough to donate an organ for the betterment of another. This night was no different; however, on this particular night, with my new bouncy short haircut, I was unaware that I would have the surprise fright of my life.

Once my instrumentation was neatly aligned on the sterile medical tray; I started by spreading the eyelids until all the edges of the round organs were visible. With the clamp firmly in place, I spoke to my charge, "Well, hello, Mr. Brown. I am sorry for your passing but appreciate your donation. A car accident I see. That sucks, matey. Well, what I can tell you on this, our first meeting? Hmmm, well, I got a new haircut today. What do you think? Do I look hot in short hair?" Just at that moment, in the cold, sterile chamber of the morgue with Mr. Brown, with the body of Mr. Brown lying on the steel slab, I was given a shock! Mr. Brown suddenly went from lying flat and lifeless to sitting straight up at a ninety-degree angle with his legs straight out in front of him. The scream I let out was so blood-curdling that I failed to recognize that it was mine.

After a few seconds, the echo of my scream brought me back to the present. I went to push the button on the wall for Joey to come, but I found I was as stiff as the stiff! I couldn't make my feet move away from the drawer slab and the body of Mr. Brown. Luckily, Joey was already on his way as he saw what happened on the monitor system in the control office. When Joey burst through the door, I was still and rigid like a corpse!

"Hey Aussie, you okay? My God, that must have spooked the bejesus out of ya, little lady!"

For the second time in my life, I was speechless. My brain

was numbed. I ran to him and hugged him so tightly I thought I might choke him to death! I was never so glad to see Joey! I just couldn't shake this unexpected experience off like a dog shakes water from its fur after a bath. It was one thing to have book knowledge that, theoretically, gasses can expel from a corpse resulting in a change of body position – but this was too much!

Joey could see I was going to faint. "Okay, Isabella. Easy there. Let's sit in this chair. I've seen this one other time before. You are going to be all right. It's sure a shocker." Joey wheeled a chair and positioned it behind my calves. He gently touched one hand on my shoulder while soothingly saying, "There you go. Sit on down now." Somehow, I managed to get my dithers together. I knew that if I was going to work in medicine that the unexpected was inevitable. I turned on my analytical brain and knew that a donor recipient was waiting. The overly responsible me could do this!

I took a few breaths while sitting down and got my mind in a better place. "Joey, it's okay. I got this."

"Are you sure? We still have time to call someone else in." Joey reassured me.

"I am positive. I was told when I was hired that I was the first girl to ever get hired. I am not going to be a wanker and wuss out. I got this – really."

"Okay, little lady, but I will just hang out with you just in case."

With that, I stood up, determined to finish my task. It was probably the quickest I ever performed the procedure. Despite a bit of slight trembling, I managed to get both eyes into the bag and immersed in the preservation solution. I kept telling myself I was a tough Aussie from the Outback, and I could finish. I filled the second bag with saline and put the first bag in the second.

Finally, the two bags were immersed in the third bag, which I also filled with saline. I was thankful that Joey stayed until I finished placing the precious eyes being donated into the small blue and white Igloo cooler. Joey completed the packing with ice and turned to go, "I must say Isabella, you are a true champ. You are going to make a great doctor one day!"

Together, Joey and I walked out of the chamber and started down the sterile hallway. By this time, I was back in charge of my emotions. I learned at an early age that controlling emotions meant survival. I called Jan and asked him to meet me at the eye bank. Luckily, he answered and agreed to come. When I told him what happened, he tried to suppress his laughter. When he no longer could, I, too, began to laugh. I laughed so hard that my stomach ached. That night I slept with the light on. Jan held me as tightly as he could without breaking my ribs. Before falling asleep, I knew that it wasn't just a change in my hairstyle; part of me changed in an inexplicable way. I wasn't sure why I felt uneasy. Tomorrow was another day. Exhausted, I fell asleep.

Chapter 9

With graduation ceremonies completed, life moved on. Sandie and I arranged to meet for a cuppa. Walking into the Wine and Cheese Nook, I saw Sandie and waved. "Hi girlfriend! I am loving this weather! How was your graduation?"

The server came, and we ordered our drinks. While Sandie took a moment to greet friends at the café, my mind was working on overdrive. I never liked the bitter taste of coffee but loved the smell. I ordered a cup of Earl Grey, and Sandie ordered a cappuccino. I marveled at how artistic the coffee cream formed a perfect four-leaf clover. My cuppa was served exactly the way I liked it! The serving board contained a built-in timer, and the pot of tea sat cozily in the rounded etched wood groves. Every time I went to a café or restaurant, I always felt lucky I never had to work in food service. I did not have the talent to graciously deal with irate customers and appease them and their various complaints. My mind wandered until I heard the light ting informing me my tea was now perfectly steeped. Just then, the delectable cheese board with various cheese and fruits was brought to the table.

"So... tell me everything! How was your graduation? C'mon, spill the beans! I have been waiting patiently for the news you wanted to share last week!" I egged Sandie on excitedly.

Sandie's face lit up. "Well, graduation was very nice. Three of my sisters put together a very nice outside barbeque. Then Patrick took me to a resort in Ocean City for two nights. I knew he was up to something when he told me to bring a nice dress. One thing he never does is suggest what I should wear."

"Ooooh la la! So…go on!" I urged her.

"It was totally unexpected! When we returned to the hotel, I felt like a character in a soppy romance novel. Patrick had scattered pink and white rose petals into a heart shape on the bed. He had chocolate-dipped strawberries and an ice bucket with champagne. Not that I was going to drink the champagne!"

"Wow! That is awesome! I always liked Patrick more than—"

"Than Amir, the Middle Easterner. I know, I know." Sandie giggled softly.

"Okay, sorry to interrupt! Please continue!"

"Well, the champagne glasses had a "Mr." and "Mrs." inscribed on them with white sparkly paint! I thought, no way, he is NOT going to propose!"

Clapping with glee, I shouted, "Yes! Did he get on one knee?"

"Yes, he DID, girlie! I couldn't believe it myself. At first, I didn't know what I would say. I considered how young we are to make a huge commitment. I also considered what would happen to my career. Let's face it, I don't know him as well as I think you should know someone before getting married."

"Go on! Don't keep me in suspense!"

Sandie held up her hand and displayed a pear-shaped diamond engagement ring. Her face was beaming! I was very happy for her. Of course, this got my mind racing again. I had hoped that Jan would not ask me to marry him for a few reasons – I wasn't ready, and he smoked too much pot.

"So, that's what you wanted to tell me when we were going to the Belvedere? That you got engaged! I am so happy for you!"

Sandie started smiling but hesitated a bit, "Well, I figured he was going to ask, but I wasn't positive. I didn't want to ruin your first ever surprise party, so I figured I would wait. Actually, I have more news."

"Oh, no! This doesn't sound good! How could your engagement ruin my surprise party? What happened? Something to your grandma? Your mom acting ridiculous again? You were accepted into the MBA program? You—"

Sandie cut me off. "No, no! It's nothing bad. At least, I hope not. Patrick and I already talked about it, and we were wondering if you would be willing to become a godmother."

Sandie's face beamed, and she started shaking her head slowly when I mumbled, "Oh my God. You are pregnant!"

"Yes! I did not really think Patrick would want to get married. That was so unexpected because he knew I was okay with living together. He is so excited about this baby. He has plenty of nieces and nephews back home in Venezuela. He is thrilled – but I am not so sure that his family shares his enthusiasm, considering I don't speak Spanish." Sandie offered more smiles.

"I am so honored to be asked! Are you sure you and Patrick want me to be the godmother? I don't know what to say!"

"Say yes!" Sandie nodded her head up and down.

"Okay, okay! Yes! I will be your child's godmother! I can't believe it! A wedding and a baby! What about you? How do you feel about all this? So much, so quickly!" I grabbed Sandie and hugged her.

"I never saw my life going this way. Of course, I will be working until the baby is born. Patrick and I are looking for an apartment. Just because I am getting engaged and going to be a mom doesn't mean you and I will stop playing tennis! I want you to know that, no matter what, you will always be welcome to stay with us. You never have to worry about being homeless. I mean that!"

With those words, I felt my eyes well up with tears of joy. I raised my cup, "To a new future and friendship forever!" We clinked our cups together and laughed like we were twelve-year-old girls making a pinky promise.

"I am not going to cry, girlfriend!" I assured Sandie. "Just so much to take in. I still can't believe you want me to be a godmother. Thank God I am older than eighteen now!" Both Sandie and I laughed.

"You are right! Oh my gosh, I totally forgot about your age! You always seem older to me than you are!"

I felt blessed to have Sandie in my life since the first day we met on the courts. I knew from the start that she and I would be great friends. Over the past four years, we found out we didn't just have tennis in common. Sandie came from a dysfunctional home; however, her older sisters, mother, and grandmother all loved her. We did have one difference which made me appreciate her even more. Unlike Sandie, my parents came from money – lots of money. Sandie's dad left when she was two years old and never came back. She and her five sisters grew up very poor. I might have been given clothes that were hand-me-downs my entire childhood that *she* purchased at Goodwill stores, but Sandie was happy to get anything "new" to her while growing up.

When I was growing up *she* dressed us in pants that were too short and outdated. The embarrassment I could overcome, the ridicule I could not. Shirts were ill-fitting, and the sleeves were always ridiculously too short to fit my long arms. I was not embarrassed only because of how I looked, but also because of the humiliation I felt as my friends knew my parents came from money. *She* always had new clothes, new precious gems, gold and diamond jewelry, new shoes, and new purses, but the three of us were given thrift store clothes.

Her rationalization for dressing us so poorly was made clear. We heard many times that we weren't deserving of anything and the phrase, "New things have to be earned." Earning was expected for everything – even basic hygiene needs. We were only allowed one shower a week and to enjoy that "privilege". When we each turned eight, we had to find a way to pay for the water, or we were denied a shower. During the week, I used to go to Mom and Dad "D"'s house after gymnastics practice to take showers and wash my hair. While I was always terrified that I might get caught, it was worth feeling clean and helped avoid being the subject of bullying. On the weekends, I was just out of luck. I knew that I would be nothing like *her* as a godmother! I was going to give my godchild sincere, pure love. I would never deny my godchild anything – emotional or material – that I was sure of!

"I still can't believe it, so much is happening so fast! You are sure you are good with all this?" I asked Sandie with true concern.

"I'm right as rain, as my mother always says," Sandie quickly assured me.

"What about planning? Oh! Who is organizing your bachelorette party?" It was obvious I couldn't contain my excitement. "A wedding and a baby, the excitement is like the reaction you get when shaking a can of seltzer water and spraying the joy of fizz when opening it!" I giggled.

"I never thought I would be getting married so young, let alone having a child. If I'm going to be honest, I never really thought about having children. I see the struggles my mother had, and still has, throughout her life," Sandie confided.

"Don't go getting all crazy and underestimate your abilities to be a mom. You will be a terrific, sensitive, understanding mom! You are smart, capable, and have a beautiful soul! Both

Patrick and your child are lucky to have you. Plus, you already have the frugal thing down pat, so that should be a snap figuring things out when finances get tight." I volunteered.

"I know. I am just hoping Patrick is up for the challenge of a wife and a baby. Plus, I told him I always envisioned myself fostering children. I never thought about having my own child. Besides the nine-month ordeal, there is the pain and terror of labor!"

"Whoa! That's a lot! Firstly, you are tough, and I know you will manage the pregnancy just fine. You also need to remember this child you are carrying will come into a world of love and be welcomed into both your lives. I will say, though, that in all fairness, let yourself and Patrick get used to having one child first before springing on your good Samaritan desires. I am sure you already earned your angel wings just taking care of your grandmother. Even though your sisters are not around, they still could have lent you a hand with your grandma."

"I know. I tried to convince Patrick we should live at my mom's house. That way finances will be a bit easier for us. Plus, I can keep helping my mom take care of my grandmother. But Patrick is set on a new place for us to start a new family. He doesn't get along that well with my mom. You know my mom can be weird about immigrants. She's not against them in any way, but she doesn't trust anyone who doesn't speak English as a first language."

"Wait a minute! That's messed up. Didn't your mom immigrate here when she was a teen?" I inquired.

"Yes, she did. She was already married to my father. Not only was he a lush, but he never paid one dime of child support. He just vanished."

"Yeah. That stinks, but I still don't see the connection with prejudice against South American immigrants."

"Oh, that's easy to explain! My lush of a father ran off with a woman from Brazil. I guess I never mentioned that before." Sandie sighed just a bit.

"Well then, that makes perfect sense. Perhaps you need to remind your mom about your ex-boyfriend and ask her if she would have preferred him to Patrick?" I said with slight sarcasm.

Sandie lightly chuckled, "For sure, because being Muslim and requiring me to wear a hijab would be so much better than being South American. My mom would totally have overlooked that Amir wanted total control of me, my finances, and decisions regarding education, and employment." Sandie shared with sarcasm. "I am sure my mom would have condoned a marriage with Amir. She thought Amir was a charmer since he was Muslim and didn't drink. That one fact alone won my mom's favor. Unfortunately, Patrick does drink, and that puts my mind on the defense. She thinks one drink is one too many after being married to an alcoholic. You know how she is, so I have to find a way to get my mom to be team Patrick!"

"I see," I giggled. "Your mom is totally justified in her thought process." I teased a bit.

Sandie and I shared our thoughts with each other about our futures. Sandie felt so secure in hers. I felt so insecure about mine. But one thing I knew was that I had to follow my heart. Despite rationalizing and intellectualizing my options, my heart always led me to a path of coaching gymnastics. Medicine could wait. My yearning to find an identity, a place, a niche in life, was a bit elusive. I knew that one day I would find it.

Chapter 10

Since our meeting at the Wine and Cheese Nook, Sandie and I had very little, if any, time to get together. She was working feverishly on wedding plans and settling into her new apartment. She and Patrick rented a two-bedroom, one bath apartment about twenty minutes out of the city. Sandie was extremely creative. The eclectic neighborhood seemed safe as it was located on the edge of a predominantly Polish neighborhood. The brick duplex housed both young families and elderly persons. It was definitely not in middle-class America, but it wasn't in a bad part of town. Sandie was not dissuaded as she knew it was temporary. She knew, within less than a year, she and Patrick would be able to afford a new place in a better neighborhood.

Until a nicer apartment was in Sandie's reach, Sandie could decorate anything with class and modern style on a dime. Sandie was the queen of "design on a dime" and "reuse and repurpose" before the notions became popular reality tv programming. Sandie also knitted. I wasn't sure if it was an obsession or an addiction. She knitted baby sweaters, mittens, tiny caps, and booties every spare minute available. Since Sandie continued working at the newspaper, we still had some time to catch up with one another. Although, it was not often that we worked the same shift, so any catch-up time was good catch-up time. While Sandie was decorating her home, working full time, and preparing for a wedding and a baby, I was sending out as many resumes as possible. I was fortunate to be able to use the computers at the newspaper and Eye Bank to compose and print cover letters and resumes. I bought professional-grade, light grey stationery that had a slight sheen to it. I thought a classic style would be best and more professional than plain white printer paper. I sent a total of a hundred resumes since I graduated. I was lucky to have received two professor references and three employer references. The most important references were that of Brent Lindi and the head of the US Gymnastics judging federation. In the past weeks, I received only three letters of interest. One in Boise, Idaho, one in En Cenada, Mexico, and one in a rural area of the Netherlands. In mulling over these choices, I knew that none of them would lead to coaching Olympic gymnasts. When I consulted with Brent Lindi, he agreed. I knew my best course of action was to hold out for a career stepping stone coaching job and just *believe*! I would follow my heart, continue to dream, and believe. After another month went by and no other plausible coaching job offers came my way, I decided to ask Lindi if he could pull some strings. After all, I was reliable, considered a good choreographer and spotter of difficult balance beam flight series and floor exercise routines. For once, having broad shoulders was a bonus! Admittedly, I wasn't as confident when it came to spotting vault and the uneven bars, but I wasn't afraid to improve. I was fearless. I also knew I was a damn good technician as a coach. I also knew how to motivate kids, and kids seemed to like me.

  I loved everything about coaching and judging. I loved the smell of the large blue and beige striped tumbling mats, the creak of the spring floor made when gymnasts were tumbling, the pouncing and pop sounds of the beat board when gymnasts' feet met the springboard when approaching the vault, and the slight tinny, clanking noise adjusting the uneven bar brackets when setting the spacing of the uneven bars. I loved participating in the warm-up and conditioning exercises with the gymnasts. I even loved the silky feel of the white powdery chalk and the slight puff of white that dispersed in the air when the girls completed the three hundred and sixty degree giants on the uneven bars. Giants always made me picture the little toy that had a bar and a monkey. When pushing the button, the monkey went around the bar in a three hundred and sixty degree circle. No matter how many times I watched a gymnast perform a giant, I still found myself smiling with delight.

There wasn't anything I didn't love about gymnastics. With my mind made up about securing a viable coaching job, I decided to call Lindi and let him know I was judging floor exercise at the upcoming regional meet. That way, he may be willing to introduce me to any Olympic coaching staffers who would be scouting for potential stars at the meet. As I neared the regional gymnastics arena, my heart started racing. Not because I was nervous about judging, but because somewhere deep inside, I knew this was my moment. Something spectacular was going to happen! I knew it with all my heart and soul. I reminded myself to be confident and bold. Sandie gave me a pep talk, and Mom "D" put her two cents in when we spoke on the phone earlier in the morning. "Don't back down, Isabella. No one got to the moon by being too afraid to try. Just say what you want and don't beat around the bush. Be confident." Mom "D" proclaimed with exuberance, "I believe in you. You need to believe in you!" Thinking about her words, I approached the vast arena with renewed confidence and determination. I checked in at the registration table, received my judging pass, which allowed me access to all the coaches and gymnasts on the arena floor, and set about finding Lindi. Finally, after an hour of looking, waving hi to gymnasts, and chatting with other judges, I spotted Lindi.

Walking across the spring floor tumbling run warm-up area, I waved and shouted, "Lindi, Gotta a quick sec?" He motioned me over.

"What's up, Pladdy?"

"Seriously, you don't think it's time to drop the Pladdy?" I teased lightly while giving Lindi a light punch on the shoulder

"Nope! Pladdy suits you. You are forever a Pladdy! So, what's going on? Your voice message mentioned me introducing you to a few scouts or gym owners. Correct?"

"Yes, that is correct. I have received a few coaching offers, but I wouldn't call them premier gymnastic destinations. Seriously, how many Olympic gymnasts ever came out of Bosie, Idaho?"

"I feel you, Pladdy. You know, since I have met you, I learned you have fierce determination and are rock solid in work ethic, coaching and judging skills. Mostly, I know if I don't help, you will never stop hunting me down until I do." Lindi smiled and put up his hand in a high five position.

I met his high five with an overly excited slap. "I am soooooo ready, Lindi." Lindi looked at me and waited a very long minute, staring at me with his hand to his chin in his thinking posture. "So – you are ready for the next level of coaching? It can get downright political, so you will have to be tough. Plus, you have to be patient. As you know, there are no top female coaches, and men have a tendency to think women coaches can't cut it. But I think when they meet you, they will see it's to their advantage to hire a female who is not just a good choreographer but also an excellent spotter and technician. Your height and broad shoulders are a bonus for sure. Having your judging experience and certifications certainly help!"

"I feel honored you feel that way about me. So, tell me when and where you want me to be whenever you are ready to help launch my career."

"There is going to be a USGA senior judge and coaching information session to discuss new optional routine guidelines after the awards ceremony. I will put your name on the registration list as my guest. Here's an official I.D. pass for entry. It's at seven p.m. sharp." I was so excited walking across the floor that I forgot to look down and tripped on a tumbling mat.

"Well, that is grace if ever I saw it," a man with a thick accent said as he reached his hand out to help me up. Embarrassed a bit, I shook it off with what I thought was a witty reply.

"G'day sir, and thank you. I may not be all things grace, and clearly that's why I'm not a rhythmic gymnastics coach. My name's Isabella." I started laughing.

"I'm Vladimir. I fear I don't get the joke. So, who are your Olympic 'wannabe's' here today?" Vladimir had a deep voice, strong hands, a clearly defined muscular tone, and an inviting smile.

"I have three gymnasts I'm rooting for as I coached them with Brent Lindi. But I am here today as a judge and not a coach, so let's keep my bias between the two of us, shall we?" I whispered and smiled.

"Of course, Ms. Isabella. I never heard any of that," he said in a joshing tone.

"What about you, Mr. Vladimir? Who are your future stars competing today? Women or men? Also, I detect an accent, and I've not seen you at any of the previous meets I've judged."

"How perceptive, indeed." Vladimir replied in a bit of a condescending tone. "I am also not coaching today. I am scouting for junior recruits who would be an asset for my country."

"And your country is?" I asked.

"Germany. You can not tell by my accent? Sprechen de Deutche, Ms. Isabella? I am guessing not as you are either from South Africa or Australia based on your accent. My money is on South Africa since you don't have blonde hair."

With that statement, I tried to hold back my sarcastic reply, but it fell out of my mouth like a baby tasting the first spoonful of puréed green peas. "I suppose you haven't heard, but the quest to build the Arian race was defeated in WWII. If you must know, I'm Australian – West Australian."

"Well, I see you have grit and a quick wit Ms. Isabella." Vladimir smiled and extended his hand. "The best to you."

With that exchange, the bell dinged to signal all persons needed to clear the arena floor. The announcer proceeded to call for all gymnasts, coaches, judges, and spectators to report to their appropriate areas.

Following the national anthem, the announcer began introducing top United States gymnastics officials. I heard the announcer state that "Today's meet is the national qualifier," and I got super excited! I went into the judges' designated room and changed into my navy blue linen suit donning the USGA patch on the upper right-hand pocket. I gathered up my point deduction "cheat sheet", double-checked my locker was locked and walked to the judges' table at the floor exercise to check in with the head judge. Once all the event judges were gathered, the head judge stated, "There were no rule changes this year, so computing each gymnast's score should go quickly. Since compulsory routines are exactly the same for each gymnast, every deduction should be easy to make. Let's not be so far apart on our final score. I like everything neat and tidy. After instructions were given, I extended my greeting to the other four familiar faces and sat down at the judging table. With the women's gymnasts' compulsory routines completed, I breathed a sigh of relief. I had been within point one to point two of the other judges' scores for each routine. I felt good about my keen eye and consistency. There would be an hour break for a quick bite before gymnasts performed their individual optional routines. Knowing these routines would be much harder to judge to stay in line with the other judges, I thought a quick bite to keep up my motivation and energy level would be in order. I retrieved the sandwich and coke I had brought with me and slipped out the back door to eat under a large maple tree in the shade.

While eating my plain Jane sandwich, my mind wandered. I thought about the absurdity of calling it women's floor exercise, as clearly the young girls competing had not yet even hit puberty. I also knew that for some of the gymnasts over ten, a growth spurt could very quickly end their careers. At the very least, a growth spurt of an extra inch or two disorients a gymnast when twisting and turning. The disorientation frequently results in under-rotated landings, broken limbs, and broken hearts. I knew that from personal experience when I was in the prime of my gymnastic career. To my surprise, while solving all the problems of the world feasting on salami and cheese, Lindi came walking toward me. "Hey Lindi. Whatcha doing slumming it with me? I do have an extra protein bar if you would like one," I offered.

"I don't always eat out, Isabella. Only ninety-five percent of the time." Lindi snickered.

"Actually, I have a coaching friend I want you to meet. His country has a spot open on their gymnastic team for a beam and floor coach. With your skills and judging credentials, you would be perfect. Wrap that lunch up and come with me." I quickly took one last bite, packed things up, and jumped up with excitement. "Is it an international team? Do they have an Olympic program?"

I asked with exuberance.

"Yup."

I followed Lindi back into the arena and walked past the inner sports offices. Lindi opened the door to a room marked 'international coaching staff and guests'.

Lindi waved, and Vladimir started to approach us. "I would like you to meet my very good friend and fellow Olympian, Vladimir Gegens." Vladimir extended his hand. "It is a pleasure to meet you again, Ms. Isabella from Australia. Correction – West Australia."

With a slightly confused stammer, Lindi piped up, "Oh, I didn't realize the two of you knew one another."

"We don't." I responded quickly. "We just met earlier… when I tripped." I blushed, looking at Vladimir, and managed to salvage, "And nice to meet you again as well, Mr. Germany."

Vladimir cheerily grinned. He had a perfect smile with perfectly aligned teeth that were blindingly bright white. "I see you and Lindi are friends. He has been singing your praises. I would like to talk with you after the meet if that's possible."

"Are you kidding? I would love that! Where in Germany is your gymnastics center?" I asked, a bit too enthusiastically.

"It's in Stuttgart. Have you heard of it?" Vladimir replied.

"Yes, I have! I know that a few Olympic gymnasts were trained there." I said with a smile.

"Well, Ms. Isabella, I need to leave you for the moment, but look forward to chatting with you after the meet. Say about six-thirty meet me back here?" Vladimir flashed his perfect white teeth.

"Absolutely!" I couldn't wait for the meet to end. I had a very good feeling that I would be invited to join the coaching group staff in Germany. I knew now, more than ever, that every routine I watched and judged had to be judged with precision and accuracy. Vladimir would surely speak with the head judge and ask how I did. I knew he would scrutinize my technical skill level proficiency. There could be no mistakes! Six p.m. felt like it would never come… I was ready.

Chapter 11

The regional gymnastic meet was over; I couldn't wait to get back to Baltimore to tell Jan the great news. Flying back from Texas gave me plenty of time to rehearse how I would break the news to Jan about my offer to coach with Vladimir in Stuttgart. I knew Jan wouldn't be thrilled with the idea. Even though we had some bumps in the road, I continued to live with him. He was completing his final year fellowship as a cranial facial surgeon. I didn't just live with him out of convenience, but because I truly loved him. I didn't love his drug habit, nor did I approve, but I loved *him*. Some would describe me as a prude. At some point, I suspected he would ask me to marry him. We were together almost five years, and for Jan, having a family and children was just the next step. That was a point on which we didn't see eye to eye. I knew I would have to pick the right moment to share my great news when I returned. I also knew there was no way to break it to him gently that I was leaving for Stuttgart in three months to coach gymnastics. The flight attendant gave the routine landing announcement. The "stay in your seats until the plane has completely stopped at the gate" might as well be, "the second the wheels hit the ground, run to the front to hurry and wait" announcement. Of course, when the plane touched down, passengers immediately jumped up before the plane was stopped and rushed to the front. Slightly annoyed, I decided that the 'me mentality' would not ruin the excitement that was still brewing. I was offered a coaching position of a lifetime! Nothing can ruin my mood, I told myself.

From the numerous plane flights, I learned to park in a 'C' lot, so I was not that person frantically holding my car remote, clicking away, looking for headlights to find my car. Happy to have found my car and toll ticket quickly, I found myself on the Jones Falls Expressway headed into the city. After a half hour of driving, cars were at a standstill. It seemed like an eternity to get through the construction zone. Daydreaming about my future journey in Germany, I was startled when the driver behind me honked impatiently. Finally, back in gear, I had to get my head in the game. Nearing the apartment, I could feel my nerves get the better of me. I knew telling Jan of my plans would be a heartbreaker for him. Upon turning the key, I heard footsteps approaching the door.

"Surprise!" Jan gleefully proclaimed. "I bet you didn't think I would be here when you got back. I know these past two years I have been more of a ghost than a partner, but here I am!"

"You are right there, Jan! So, no, actually I thought you would be at the hospital, but I'm glad you are here. I've so much to tell you!"

"Well, before you do, why don't you shower and settle in? I've made reservations for dinner at your favorite Indian restaurant."

"Wow! Is it a special occasion I don't know about?" I asked with a bit of edginess in my voice. I felt like I was going to burst any second if I didn't get out my news.

Before Jan could answer, a small, pure white kitten with one green and one blue eye appeared from behind the couch and gave a quiet meow while butting his head against my calf.

"Oh my gosh, who is this little cutie?" I asked, kneeling down to let the kitten get acquainted with my scent.

"That's Jasper. I agreed to cat sit for one of the resident interns at the hospital. Don't get too excited. We are not keeping him." Jasper arched his back and tilted his head slightly upward so I could scratch his chin. His fur was pure white, medium length, and very soft. He had one blue eye and one green eye. What kind of name is Jasper for a cat? I would have named him 'Sprite'," I proclaimed.

"I agree, he is definitely a Sprite," Jan nodded. "I've got to run some errands. Reservations are for six forty-five. I'll be back in time to get a quick shower before we go."

Hearing the door open, little 'Sprite' ran to the door. "Oh no, little one, you are staying here with me," I declared firmly while scooping up the sweet ball of fur, watching Jan back out the VW. I had forgotten how fun having a furry companion actually was. "I am officially changing your name to Sprite. What do you think about that?" As if the cat would actually answer.

"Okay, Sprite, time for me to get ready for dinner," I whispered. While showering, I decided the best approach to breaking my news about Germany was to wait until after Jan and I got back from dinner. I didn't want to muck the waters and ruin any plans he might have made. Showered, I spent a bit of time playing with Sprite, all the while remembering Suki. I hoped she was pouncing mice somewhere in cat heaven. I made a mental note to look into if Germany had ample cat and dog-friendly apartments. The past year, Jan and I rarely had the same schedule. This enabled Jan to be a slacker when it came to household chores. He knew that when we did have time together, I wouldn't waste time nagging him about chores. Besides, I knew he was never going to do them anyway. I threw some laundry in the washer and then went to my closet to decide on an outfit. I wanted to wear something feminine but not too sexy. I didn't want Jan to get too hopeful we might have sex after dinner. We hadn't had sex for a while, and I didn't want to get distracted from telling him my great news. Then again, reconsidering, telling him at dinner, would most definitely dampen the romantic mood.

I settled on a classically styled, tan khaki wrap dress and a pair of light orange one-inch heels. Being post-platypus, it was amazing any dress shoes fit my ever-widening and flattening feet. While I never had glass slipper-type feet, after the rugby accident, the glass slipper was definitely a fairy tale. Looking fantabulous from the ankles up would have to do!

"There, Sprite! Perfect," I said, looking in the mirror with confidence. I wore a fresh pearl slip-on bracelet and a blue topaz, pear-shaped pendant necklace with matching earrings. I didn't have many clothes or expensive jewelry. When I did splurge, I chose only classically designed pieces to weather the test of time. It was Jenny who taught me how to look for stylish, clean-lined, simple pieces to add to my wardrobe. Because of my childhood clothing experiences, I refused to wear anything from a thrift store, but I was the 'Queen of Clearance'. I heard the VW pull up outside and park in the driveway. We were lucky to have a driveway attached to the apartment in the city. I opened the door and greeted Jan with a warm welcome of a hug and a kiss. "Right on time! I'm looking forward to chicken tiki masala and naan," I blurted out a bit nervously. Jan jumped in the shower and was dressed in a flash.

His mood seemed light. "Your chariot awaits, my dear. You look great, as always."

"Well, thank you, my liege, and you do as well," I said, stepping over the marble door threshold. As I was about to get into the VW, Jan ran ahead and opened the door.

"Hmmmmm," I pondered, "All this pomp and circumstance. Is there something special going on I should know about?"

"Nope. Just my normal charming and dapper self, taking my sexy girlfriend to dinner." He smiled, shut my door, and put the clutch in gear.

"Wow, Jan. Flattery will get you everywhere," I responded, silently wishing he was not going to be this charming the rest of the night because that would make it more difficult to tell him my news. I could definitely tell he was up to something but wasn't sure what. On the way to the restaurant, our conversation was shallow, expressing mundane aspects of work. Jan and I used to talk about everything, but no longer. We used to share simple observations, such as "Why do you need more than eight pairs of underwear when there is only seven days in a week?" or "Why ask everyone how they are doing when there was no interest in knowing how the person was – now – or ever."

The VW came to a halt in front of Indian Palace. "Isabella, let them know we are here while I park. I don't want to lose our reservation."

Jan's request reminded me of how cheap – okay, frugal – he could be. While Jan claimed he never used the valet because he didn't want them to ruin his VW, I knew better. Sitting at the table, I quickly ordered appetizers before Jan could change his mind.

"It seems forever since we had time to relax and have a date," Jan offered, starting the conversation. Things between us over the years became too comfortable in many ways. Jan already treated the "us" as being married. Romantic gestures were long gone. This was disconcerting, and I knew that if I married Jan, I would have to accept that niceties would be far and few between.

"I know. I feel the same. How has work and the fellowship been going? Any interesting surgical cases?" I asked in an attempt to continue the easy flow of conversation.

"You know, the same. It's so political working in a hospital. I don't know if I am up for being a cut throat. I know that's not me. I don't want to be 'that guy'," Jan replied with a hushed sigh.

"What do you mean, 'that guy'?" I asked with sincerity.

"The guy who treats colleagues like shit just to get ahead. I never imagined working in dental medicine would feel like the Tasmanian Devil versus Daffy Duck," Jan said with a slight smile.

I wanted to ask Jan if he was the Tasmanian Devil or Daffy Duck, but I didn't dare. Instead, I commented empathetically, "I can't imagine what you are facing, but I do know what it's like being in a political arena when I am judging gymnastics."

"Please, Isabella, you aren't actually comparing a silly judging job to dentistry. Really?" Jan asked with a dismissive tone.

"That is a bit harsh, Jan, but I am willing to overlook it as I know you have been very stressed," I quickly retorted.

Feeling deflated and insulted, I gave Jan the benefit of the doubt. His work hours were brutal, and he did not like confrontation. I knew he was not cut out for the stress of politics in any job. He definitely didn't like jockeying for power in a work situation.

"I'm sorry, Isabella. I wanted this to be a nice dinner between us. I have something to share with you, and I hope you will be on board."

My mind went into overdrive. "On board?" This did not sound like a lead up to a proposal.

"Well, that's not a hopeful start. I have news to share with you too, but maybe it's best for you to go first and say what's on your mind." I quickly stated.

Just at that moment, the server came to take our order.

"I'm breaking my own rules about drinking – I think I am going to need it for this conversation. I will have a sauvignon blanc, please. What about you, Jan?"

"What? You are ordering wine? I never thought I would see

the day! I will have a beer, preferably a Stella if you have it." Jan seemed pleased I was drinking with him.

Chuckling, I thought it best to be clear. "Don't get too excited. I will only have one glass of wine." With our drink orders in, I timidly explored the reason why we were on a date since it was such a rarity. "So… you have some news? Did you get a job offer in another state? Are you thinking about buying a house? I am all ears!"

"You know I love you, Isabella. I have since the day I laid eyes on you. We have had our ups and downs, but I can't imagine not having you in my future."

My mind went into overdrive. Starting any conversation with a love declaration could either be followed by a magical or a not-so-magical moment. Jan's eyes gleamed with happiness as he spoke. I was leaning toward a not-so-magical, maybe even dreaded moment. I felt my nerves start to rattle as I feared he was going to ask me to marry him. Part of me was excited, as this would be my first proposal, but the other part of me knew I was not going to give up my dream job in Stuttgart. Bracing for the big question, I took a sip and blurted out, "I can't marry you. I am going to take a job in Stuttgart, Germany, as a gymnastics coach for Junior Olympians and Olympic hopefuls." So much for my plan to break it to him gently.

The air became thick with tension, and Jan's expression was not what I expected. In fact, Jan began laughing. The type of laugh that indicates one is relieved. The kind of laugh that says, "Whew, I dodged a bullet with that response." I watched Jan silently pick up his Stella, waiting for him to reply. Putting his beer back on the table, he took my hand and said, "I wasn't going to ask you to marry me. I was going to tell you I am going to move back in my parent's house to help out my Dad since he needs more help these days. I was going to ask if you wanted to move in with me. We can use the back guesthouse. My Dad is getting older and got a diagnosis of colon cancer. I can't abandon him or my mom right now."

Flabbergasted, I tried to catch my breath. "That is what you wanted to tell me?" I stammered while my face turned a few shades of red.

Jan slowly nodded his head as he waited for the fullness of my reaction. After gathering my thoughts, I looked at Jan and started laughing at myself. "I am a complete idiot. I made myself sick over telling you about accepting my job offer! I thought, well, of course, I… who wouldn't think that… that this was a special dinner for a special occasion? Especially, when your idea of eating out is getting your mom's left overs."

At that moment, despite already knowing, I reminded myself that life is never predictable. I was angry at myself for thinking, just for a second, that life could be a fairy tale. But even then, I knew I wasn't being fair, as I had no intention of staying. Why I was so upset was tough for me to decipher with only one glass of sauvignon blanc. There was no Aladdin's lamp, no frogs to kiss, no magic potion to wake me up from a long sleep. I would have to chase my dreams alone. Despite planning on moving from Maryland to coach, knowing that Jan's big announcement was not a marriage proposal stuck like a dagger in my heart. I had no response to Jan's unexpected that he was moving into his parents' house. The rest of the dinner comprised of either silence or awkward conversation. This was most likely the last dinner Jan and I would have as a couple. My gut was sending me messages, and this time, I had no choice but to listen.

Chapter 12

I watched raindrops gently hitting the maple tree leaves. The rhythmic drip against the windowpane gave me comfort. Sprite seemed to be a permanent visitor. Jan shared that Sprite needed a new home. The time required at the hospital fellowship was all-consuming, and Sprite's human Dad felt it wasn't fair to the four-footed ball of fluff. Jan could not take Sprite because Jan's mother was allergic to pet hair. I told Jan that I would take Sprite to Germany. Today, Sprite had a vet check-up and would get his shots so I could get Sprite approved for air travel.

Watching the rain continue to drum against the window, thoughts flooded my mind. My path from West Australia to this moment was eventful. Twists and turns did not break my spirit – I had emerged a better person. I was determined to land my dream job. Thinking of my coaching job in Germany, excitement and nerves filled my heart and soul. The feelings felt surreal, as if I was experiencing deja vu. Years passed since those same feelings engulfed me when I entered college. Now, I was about to leave this part of my journey behind. Today was the last day I would be looking at the maple tree branches with rain-soaked leaves that tapped the living room windows as if to say, "Look over here." When, or if, I was coming back to Maryland was uncertain.

I understood why Jan felt compelled to move back to his parents' house, but I was not ready to join him. Not only wasn't I ready to get married, but I also knew I could not put my dreams on hold. I had to pursue my dreams, wherever that took me. Jan's parents paid for all of his schooling, and he had a great relationship with them. His parents were very nice people. I tried to be involved with Jan's parents, but I still felt uncomfortable around them. Hell, I felt uncomfortable around anyone's parents. I was ready to grow up, grow emotionally, grow professionally, and grow spiritually.

Like all growth spurts, there was pain. I drove the Ghia out of the apartment garage down Baltimore's city streets one last time to say goodbye to Ryk and Jenny. Sprite was in his carrier in the passenger's seat, screaming wildly at first. Apparently, Sprite was not a fan of being a passenger. By the time I reached the cemetery, the rain had stopped. A beautiful double rainbow greeted the living and the dead. "Did you find the pot of gold? I'm about to spread my wings again so I can use all the confidence you can give me. Okay? Look, I brought a little friend with me. His name is Sprite," I whispered while placing a bird's feather atop Ryk's gravestone.

I got in the Ghia and set the course for the resting place of my friend, Jenny. "C'mon Sprite, we have to say goodbye to Jenny, so please keep down your vocal protests!" Once I arrived at the Memorial Park, I found my way to Jenny's memorial stone. I placed white roses in front of Jenny's gravestone and tied them with a classic red plaid ribbon. Feeling a bit silly, I shared my thoughts with Jenny. "Your parents looked good considering, when I saw them a few weeks ago with Beaner. What do you think, Jen? Am I going to make it? A sign would be nice. You taught me so much about grace and dignity so don't steer me wrong now! Also, I want you to meet my new furry friend. This here is Sprite. He is a talker – like his mom. Don't forget to send me a sign." With that, I picked up Sprite's crate and found myself walking away.

Setting Sprite's crate back into the Ghia and driving out of the graveyard gates felt final. Yet, somehow, speaking to the dead felt cathartic. Without warning, tears trickled down my cheeks. Processing the enormity of my experiences in America hit me in totality. Suddenly, I had a keen yearning for an Australian meat pie. It was comfort food for me, like turkey on an open-faced sandwich smothered in gravy. Back in West Australia, there was nothing better than pulling into a petrol station and getting a home meat pie. I laughed out loud when I thought about how I bought a dozen meat pies before getting on the plane to the States. They were even good cold! So much had changed since I left Wadda, Scottie, and Stevie behind. Now I would be leaving others behind but not the memories. Thank God for my new traveling companion, Sprite!

I spent the hour drive back into the city deep in thought. When I arrived at the restaurant, I felt like I did so with my brain on autopilot. I found a parking space quickly. I was late for lunch with Morgan and Beaner.

"Well, look who it is. You are a sight for sore eyes my friend. Were you crying?" Beaner asked.

"Thanks, Beaner – and you look fantastic too!" We all laughed.

"We took a chance and ordered you a Diet Coke. It was a toss-up between tea and coke. Oh, I didn't know we were hosting a feline friend!" Morgan pointed to Sprite's carrier.

"Thanks, you two! Yeah, Sprite is coming with me to Germany. His owner wanted to rehome him. I just got back from saying my farewells at the cemetery. On the way over here from the cemetery, I thought about so many things we all have been through together."

"Oh my gosh, me too! I was thinking about the time you had

$2.00, and we went through the McDonald's drive-through." Morgan could barely get the words out. "And you were so panicked and started throwing all the packets of ketchup and sauces back into the drive-through window! That poor guy had no idea what was going on!"

Beaner, laughing hysterically, managed to get her two cents in. "Oh yeah! You were almost in tears screaming, 'I only have $2.00. I can't pay for this'!"

The three of us couldn't stop laughing. Trying to get my composure and my breath, I managed to say, "You have no idea how terrified I was. You can imagine all those condiments in the bag. If I would have had to pay twenty-five or fifty cents a packet like in Australia, it would have cost a fortune that I just didn't have! Sprite, don't listen to these ladies – it wasn't that funny." With that, Sprite meowed softly. Feeling bad Sprite was kept out of the conversation, I took him out of his carrier, and he snuggled on my lap.

"We didn't know what was going on with you that night, but it sure was funny! Remember, Jenny was laughing so hard, she couldn't even order! I don't think any of us will ever forget that!"

"Gosh, yeah. Remember how terrified you were with Jenny when she returned her shirt at the store! Another 'Aussie-ism' we didn't know would send you running! When you hid behind the column near the cash register, we had no idea what you were doing. We just figured every country lets you take back anything that doesn't fit, or you decide you don't need. Jenny told me she thought you lost your marbles when you ran behind the column and tried to hide!"

"Thanks so much for keeping that embarrassing moment alive for me, Morgan. When the cashier called the security guard, and I saw him coming toward me, I thought I was going to jail.

And the whole time, the cashier just thought I was some kind of wack job or pervert hiding behind the column!"

"Anymore 'remembers' you two would like to share before this lunch is over?" I said, laughing lightly.

"Oh, we had a crazy four years! There is that one time when you finally got your Mustang and took us all for a ride…" Morgan looked at Beaner, and they exclaimed in unison, "On the wrong side of road!"

"Well, mates, that was a cultural hiccup. But I never got a ticket – unlike one of us sitting here right now!" I winked at Beaner.

"Are you talking to me?" Beaner asked jokingly.

"Yes, speed demon! You are dangerous on the road! I totally agree with Isabella when it comes to that, Beaner. I still get nervous driving with you." Morgan showed her solidarity.

"C'mon now. We all know who was the worst driver by far!" Beaner retorted.

With that comment, we all looked at each other and said, "RYK!" and we all laughed simultaneously.

"Jesus, he was the absolutely worst driver. I am surprised he never wrapped that Shelby around a tree the way he drove. He sure knew how to live life and then some," Morgan reflected.

Suddenly, all became quiet as the irony of Ryk's driving habits comment and the cause of his death hit us. No one spoke. The silence was deafening. What seemed like an eternity finally passed as Beaner looked at us – really looked at us – and slowly shook her head as if she was still in disbelief about Ryk's fate.

"You know we had a good run. Beaner, you put up a great fight after that accident. You are my hero for sure," I offered.

With that, the silence seemed endless until Morgan affirmed my conviction. "I agree with Isabella. I don't know if I could have gotten through that time if it wasn't for your resilience and faith that you were gonna make it back a hundred percent."

During our chat, Sprite was a perfect cat. After reminiscing about teachers, road trips, and team events, it was time for Sprite's vet appointment. "Well, ladies. It's about that time. Sprite has a vet appointment. We need to get his travel certificate. Then I have to drive to Jan's house. He is driving me to the airport tomorrow, and I am leaving my Ghia with him."

"Are you sure this is what you want, Isabella? Leaving Jan and your friends? Oh, gosh, what about your cousin?" Beaner questioned, bringing her eyebrows together in scrutiny.

"Beaner, you of all people, know that you have to go after your dreams. I am ready to do that. I have youth on my side, and I can't wake up ten years from now as a dentist's wife and realize I let myself down! And just to put the record straight, I really tried to embrace Danny, but he was not an easy person to live with. I feel badly we couldn't maintain a relationship, but I guess coming from two very different dysfunctional families is an inevitable train wreck."

"One last *cheers* then!" Morgan proclaimed. With that, Howard came into view, crossing the street toward the café!

"Hey, Pladdy! Did you think you were going without a goodbye?"

"Howard! I am so glad you could make it. It seems like ages since we all got together! Meet Sprite. He is my adventure companion. We were all just about to make one more toast as I need to get Sprite to the vet!"

"Well, I know if Ryk and Jenny were here, they would be proud of you. It takes guts to take a risk and leave for another country. You got moxy, Isabella!"

With that, we all raised our glasses. "To the Sensational

Seven," we all proclaimed. Calling the vet's office, I was able to push Sprite's appointment a later hour.

"Okay, so I have one more hour as the vet could change appointment. So, Howard what's going on with you? I know I haven't seen nor heard from you in a while."

With that, Beaner and Morgan nodded their heads in agreement.

"Nothing much. I am still running the radio station and accepted a job as Director of Activities at the university."

"What? Director of Activities! That's great. You are going to be awesome in that job. I am guessing there's going to be a lot more sports activities?" Beaner asked.

"You know it, Beaner! My first love is sports, and my second is music. I don't ever feel I can fill Ryk 's shoes at the radio station, but I know I can make my mark as Activities Director. I hope to bring something fresh. You feeling me?" Howard asked, using the voice and intonation of Ryk to make his point.

All three of us bobbed our heads up and down in unison, looking like the little bobbleheads people put on the dashboard of their cars.

"Well, cheers to Howard!" I said with enthusiasm, lifting my glass.

"I got the next round," Howard spoke up and motioned the waitress to come over. "Isabella, are you going to celebrate with us? One glass of wine won't hurt."

"Okay, but make it a wine spritzer so it's not too much alcohol. You know I don't drink much and am a lightweight. I actually had two glasses of wine not too long ago!"

Morgan's eyes got big and teased, "Wow! It's a blooming miracle. You are going to have a real drink with us! Those Germans are never going to be able to compete with you in drinking games!"

Everyone laughed. Then silence. It was definitely odd having everyone together – except Jan – reminiscing without Ryk and Jenny.

"Okay, everyone, no long faces! This is a happy occasion! Thinking about drinking games – remember that time we played quarters, and Isabella refused to drink when someone got the quarter in the glass and picked her!" Beaner insisted.

"How can we forget? That was the first time I ever heard of a 'designated drinker' rule!" Morgan chuckled.

"I told you, that's Aussie rules!" I exclaimed. "Sprite, hold your ears. Your mommy plays fairly."

"I don't know about fair," Beaner chided, "but you definitely had some skills for quarters and beer pong. Who ever heard of an Aussie not liking beer, anyway?"

Conversation blathered on for the rest of the hour. The banter was always quick-witted and fun when we were all together. Finding friends came easily to me, but I had learned finding good people was not easy. I knew I was going to miss *these* people. At that moment, I realized that I wasn't as alone as I had thought – I had good friends.

"It's about that time. No long goodbyes. I mean it," I said sternly as I scooped up Sprite and put him back in his carrier.

We all hugged and hugged again. I was on the cusp of a new life. Beaner was going to pursue a master's degree in sports medicine, and Morgan was pursuing a CPA. Howard would surely make an excellent Activities Director. On the way to the vet, I again thought about the many experiences in my four years. What was around the corner was the unknown. One thing I did know was that I couldn't stay in Maryland.

Chapter 13

Standing in the airport security line, I felt calm. In truth, the totality of leaving didn't quite catch up with me as I was so busy with goodbyes and packing. The visit to Jan's was a bit more awkward than expected. I was grateful that Jan was willing to keep my car as I wasn't sure when or if I would have it shipped overseas. There was no animosity between Jan and me; there was still only love and respect. We were in different phases of our lives. It was that simple.

There was no doubt in my mind that Jan's mom was glad to see me out of the picture. She was a true mother bear, always protecting her cub. She clearly conveyed that I was breaking Jan's heart by leaving for Germany. She emphasized her point, speaking rapidly in Polish with facial expressions of disgust. If only she knew that her perfect, angelic doctor son was a pothead, she might have thought twice about being an Ice Queen. Now, standing in line, waiting to have my belongings x-rayed, none of this was my concern. I was moving on with Sprite. Fortunately, Sprite's mild sedative was working, and the security routine did not arouse him in his carrier.

Carry-on luggage stored, I sat and tucked Sprite's carrier under my seat. Watching fellow travelers boarding, I kept my fingers crossed that I would not be spending eight hours with someone smelling of garlic and taking both armrests or a body spilling over into my seat. A burly, bearded thirty-something man covered with tattoos adorning both his arms stopped at my seat row. I took a deep breath, hoping this was not going to occupy the middle seat. I relaxed when he pointed to the aisle seat and said, "Cute kitty."

Luckily, the middle seat remained open, and tattoo man loved Sprite. Sprite seemed quite comfortably settled in his carrier on the middle seat. The standard take-off formalities over, I watched the world disappear. Below, the houses looked like a monopoly board. Slowly, the world faded away, and my wheels would not stop turning. Funny how transitioning from one country to another stirred up memories and feelings. During the flight, I thought about how I was so focused on my goal when going to college. Now, I had a new goal that was going to require equal focus.

Before leaving Maryland, I lunched with Sandie. The topic of taking risks arose. I never thought of myself as a risk-taker, but then again, as a child, every day was a risk. Turning the front entry doorknob was a daily risk – *she* would either be in monster mode, or the Monster appeared shortly thereafter. Yup, I was well prepared for risks, but this wasn't risky – it was an opportunity.

Two movies and one nap later, I watched the plane's wing flaps move into position and heard the wheels groan into position for landing. I held my breath for a quick second when the wheels touched down on the runway. I arrived. I was ready for the next step in my journey. I was confident and focused. A new life was dawning, and I only had to grasp it.

Waiting at the baggage claim turnstile, Sprite protested softly with each clunk and creak of the silver luggage metal belt twirling around the carousel. I spotted my black suitcases, covered with shiny large pink and white polka dots, and dragged them off the carousel. With my suitcases and Sprite in tow, I found the ground transportation location. I scanned the various signs from numerous drivers and sighed with relief when I saw "Notski" in big, bold letters with a silhouette of a gymnast on a balance beam. Excitedly, I ran over and, in my best German, introduced myself and Sprite. To my horror, the welcome to Germany was not so welcoming for Sprite. My driver, Bruno, annoyingly growled that he was happy to transport me and my bags, but not my cat! Unfortunately, Vladimir did not check to be sure the hired driver was not allergic to cats. With my mouth gaping open, I was speechless as he said, "Find new driver!" in English!

"Well, fucking welcome to you too!" I muttered to myself while trying to flag down a taxi. Three taxis later, I found a driver willing to take Sprite and me to our new home! "G'day! Sprechen sie Englisch?" I asked the tall, dark, handsome man behind the wheel.

"Yah. Some English. My name Yavuz. Where you go?" he asked

"Here, I have it written down," I said and handed him the words '438 Stenstraus'. It's in Odesfelt."

"Ah, yah. Okay."

I could see his beautiful smile in his rearview mirror. "Are you from Germany?" I cautiously asked.

"No, Turkey," he replied.

"I feel better now!" I laughed lightly. "Being a foreigner is tough in any country."

"Where you from before?" Yavuz asked

"Oh, I moved from United States in Maryland."

"Why you come here?"

"I am teaching gymnastics at Vladimir Gymnastic Academy. Do you know it?" I chatted nervously.

"Yah. My daughter take class there. You no sound

American." He smiled.

"Really? What's her name?"

"Betula, she six." He beamed proudly

"I see! I will look for her… and you!"

Yavuz became quiet as he expertly negotiated the windy brick paver streets into the small town of Odesfelt. The large, grey stone buildings lining the streets definitely said, "Europe." The ornate cement work along roof lines and windowsills, gargoyles sitting atop large government-looking buildings, and a beautiful, lush green park that was pristine, were welcomed sites. Finally, at the top of a hill, Yavuz announced, "Here," and pulled the car over in front of a two-story, grey stone townhome. Yavuz kindly retrieved my luggage and took it to the front door. I paid and generously tipped him and promised I would look out for his daughter when I started coaching.

I rummaged in my rucksack and found the key that Vladimir had mailed to me earlier while I was still in the States. I knew no coaches would be home as it was four-thirty p.m., and competitive gymnastic practice was daily from four to nine. I took a deep breath, turned the key, and opened the door. "Well, Sprite, let's see our new home!" My first impression was, "No way! This is not Cousin Danny all over again!" I was assaulted with the stale smell of sweat, dirty shirts on the floor and furniture, and lack of cleaning in the kitchen and bathroom. Yes, one bathroom for two male coaches and myself. I told myself this was no biggie; it was all fixable! "C'mon Sprite, let's see our room and get your litter box and food and water set up."

Opening my bedroom door, I was grateful to see I had a huge window and tile floors. Tile floors were much better hygienically when having a pet. After getting Sprite out of the carrier and setting up his space, I took a much-needed thirty-minute nap. I was going to be picked up by one of the coaches in an hour and given a tour of the gymnastics academy. Guessing that the stereotype of German precision was not a stereotype, I made sure I was ready when Michilio came in the house.

"Hello, you must be Isabella. I am Michilio. Nice to meet you. Vladimir didn't tell me you are so pretty."

"Well, nice to meet you too, Michilio. I don't think I said your name correctly. And thank you for the compliment. Did he also tell you I didn't come alone?" I asked.

"Many call me Mitch. It's easier. What do you mean you didn't come alone?"

With that, I walked into my bedroom and picked up Sprite. "Meet Sprite! Sprite meet Mitch. Sprite's a cool little dude," I reassured Michilio.

"Well, well. He probably has a few good tumbling moves of his own! Maybe he can be our mascot. I love animals."

"Whew, because that is a relief, mate! The driver Vladimir sent to pick me up at the airport refused to take him in the car. He claimed he was allergic, but I think he was full of it and just disliked cats."

"Oh no! You must be industrious because you got yourself here! Well, we better get going – don't wanna be late."

The drive in the company van was only fifteen minutes. Realizing I could get around on a bike or scooter was comforting. I would not have to ask Jan to send my car overseas. There was a train system that allowed everyone to access town, a bus system, and there was Michillio's extra Vespa scooter, graciously offered. That was a relief. Along the way, there were many quaint, small shops selling baked goods, apparel, linens, shoes, flowers, groceries, and vegetable and fruit markets. These stores were like those I had pictured in a small German town.

"Here we are, Isabella," Michilio stated. "Vladimir's pride and joy. I'll introduce you to everyone and give you a tour."

Walking into the Academy, I felt at home. The twenty-five thousand square foot facility was split into two sections – a competitive and recreational section. Each section boasted the latest block spring floor tumbling area, reflex balance beams, Australian trampolines and pits, vaulting and pommel horses, uneven bars, men's high bar, and rings. The space was certainly fit to host junior Olympic hopefuls, nationally ranked gymnasts, as well as recreational wannabe gymnasts. I couldn't wait to get started. I watched some gymnasts practicing their flight series on the balance beam. When I said "hello" in my best German with an accent, Michilio laughed and let me know that most of the gymnasts spoke English. I was sensing my German was not the best.

Across the gym, I watched another coach and guessed that was my second roommate. Mitch gave the introductions. "Isabella, this is Roberto." Before me was the physique of a man who resembled a Greek god. His chiseled body oozed sex appeal. Reaching for my hand, Roberto kissed it and said, "Please, Isabella, call me Rob or Robbie. You are a welcome addition to our staff. I can feel it. Plus, I have heard all good things from Vladimir and Brent Lindi."

At that moment, Vladimir walked in the back entrance of the gym. His smile was broad as he waved enthusiastically. "Welcome, Isabella!" he called out. His warm welcome was reassuring. "I trust your flight was good. My apologies about the driver. I had no idea he was so against cats. He claims he is allergic. Please, accompany me to the office, and I can acquaint you with our policies. Can I offer you a drink?"

"Oh, no worries about the driver. I managed. I am so excited to be here! I can't thank you enough for this opportunity. I have dreamt my entire life of teaching Olympic gymnasts."

"Well, one step at a time. I would like you to shadow Robbie this week to get the lay of the land. How does that sound?"

"Perfect!" I replied with sincerity.

"Okay, well here are some human resource matters you need to attend to before tomorrow. So, why don't you shadow Robbie afterward with the optional team this evening?"

"Again, that's great!" I eagerly responded.

"Well, I will leave you to it. I am on my way out the door. See you tomorrow," Vladimir yelled as leaving the office.

Waving goodbye to Vladimir, I set to complete the human resource tasks. Once finished, I approached Robbie on the floor exercise tumbling run. "G'day again, Robbie. Vladimir wants me to shadow you this evening."

"Absolutely, Isabella. Are you comfortable spotting elite tricks like giants on the high bar and 1 1/2 layout twists and double back tucks? You look pretty strong for a girl." He chided a bit.

"You did not just say, 'for a girl!'" I giggled like a schoolgirl and found my face flush. I scolded myself for acting like a sixteen-year-old schoolgirl with a crush. I couldn't help but imagine myself with Robbie in one of those Irish Spring soap shower commercials where the man scrubs all over, smiling. I laughed at myself.

"That was supposed to be a compliment," Robbie confessed teasingly.

"Oh, I accept all compliments. Flattery will get you everywhere." I giggled. Fearful I would make a fool of myself, I quickly refocused and attended to the gymnasts' floor routines. Robbie was a skilled technician and seemed as if he had a good rapport with the team girls. I also learned quickly that he had an impatient side when excellence was not met.

The remainder of the evening went quickly. Forgotten sweatshirts, uneven bar grips, and shoes picked up off the gym floor, the three of us turned off the lights and piled into the van. Discussion of house rules seemed to be in order; however, it did not feel like the correct time driving back home. Instead, I breeched the topic of house rules, house cleaning, groceries, and meals. It was decided that buying groceries would continue to be each roommate's responsibility. All agreed that the house could be cleaned weekly and to be more conscientious about leaving smelly laundry about.

Upon arrival, Sprite ran into the living room to greet us. "Robbie, meet Sprite," I said, anxiously awaiting Robbie's reaction to Sprite. To my delight, Robbie slowly approached Sprite and let Sprite get acquainted with him. He petted him gently behind his ears and under his chin.

"Isabella, Sprite is a cutie just like you," Robbie graciously announced. "I trust he will be good company for all of us!"

I was thrilled. Things were looking up. I also noted that I had to be more astute, learning how to work with men in a household. As I had lived alone for so long, having any roommate was difficult. Having a male roommate was, admittedly, daunting. Especially roommates with whom I would work and live! Despite having a brother, I learned nothing about dealing with boys or men. I attributed my lack of male understanding to that of my father's behavior with my mother before and after his life-altering accident.

When I was nearing eight years old, my father suffered a tragic accident. On the Monday before the accident, new carpeting was installed on the steps leading to his office in the basement. In all respects, his office was his man cave. I believed he buried himself there to avoid dealing with *her* on a daily basis. If he wasn't away working or traveling, he could only be found in his cave. This particular day, it was raining very heavily, and he had worn brand new, perfectly-shined black dress shoes. I remember it like it was yesterday. He entered the living room, full of plastic-covered furniture on which we were forbidden to sit, and headed toward the hallway to his retreat. He was not able to escape to his office before having her scream the edict, "Don't think you are going sailing today!" in her raspy but shrill voice. With her words, he quickly pivoted on his slippery wet soles and lost his footing. Within that second, life completely and utterly changed. My father tumbled down the spiral, newly-carpeted staircase, landing at the bottom with his feet above his head. His head had cracked open and bright red oozed from his skull.

Looking at him lying there, I remember my curdling scream. *She* did not move a muscle. *She* just watched, saying nothing – doing nothing. At eight years old, I saw what was the third layer of the brain. When I flew down the stairs, his only words were, "Turn my legs around." *She* didn't help. *She* just stood at the top of the stairs watching. I struggled to reposition him and get his legs from above his head to the same plane as his head. His right arm had twisted a hundred and eighty degrees with his ulna sticking straight out, poking through his skin. I screamed to her to get help. *She* still stood and did nothing. I got up, ran out the back basement door, and found myself beating on a neighbor's door, screaming, "*She* will let him die." When the neighbor opened the door and heard my panicked recount of my father's predicament, he called the ambulance.

When the ambulance was leaving, I was directed by her to "clean up the mess". That night, around four a.m., she returned to the house. She dragged me out of bed by the arm, and forcefully led me down the two flights of stairs, all the while yelling, "The blood is still there – clean it right." Cleaning until she was satisfied, it was time for me to go to school. Her last words as I shut the door were "…and do not say a word to anyone."

For almost a year, myself and my siblings pretended nothing was wrong. After several brain surgeries and a brain plate insertion, he came home. He had come back in a physical body that no longer looked damaged. Little did I realize at that time that he suffered from severe traumatic brain injury. From that point on, any hope of his intervention from her daily brutal physical and mental savagery on a daily basis was forever lost. My father became extremely quiet, unopinionated, and secluded in his cave. He had no effect, and she now had supreme authority and rule. In retrospect, the mere fact he survived was a blessing, as the alternative would have most certainly meant extreme unbearable living conditions for myself and my siblings.

Upon his return, myself and my siblings dubbed our parents "the whip and the wimp". Having had pre-med and speech and language therapy college coursework, I intellectually understood how gravely my father's accident impacted his emotional and psychological intelligence. Perhaps that is why I chose Jan. He mirrored the same passivity my father displayed. Jan was not spineless when it came to his mother's wishes, but he did acquiesce without comment. Now, faced with strong-willed men, I didn't know how to navigate the waters. Nor did I know how to be a soft, delicate woman, so my new living situation was sure to be challenging.

Chapter 14

It had been two years of working with Vladimir and learning to live with two men. For the most part, things were going well. I was putting in my time and paying my dues coaching the non-competitive exhibition team. While sitting in the gym staff lounge, eating a Snickers bar, and drinking a coke to mark my two-year anniversary, I could no longer ignore that my enthusiasm and confidence for coaching were waning. The hard reality that I would not be coaching elite gymnasts any time soon conjured up a bit of quiet laughter while swallowing a mouthful of coke. I was becoming restless.

When I first arrived, I was full of myself and overconfident. I thought I was special. I was wrong. After my first week of orientation to the gym and the various recreational and competitive programs, Vladimir shattered my expectations and high aspirations. At the start of week two, I went to Vladimir's office, feeling sure he was going to place me with the nationally ranked gymnasts. Vladimir spoke glowingly of my technical and spotting abilities and commented on how well I worked with the recreational gymnastics. As he continued showering me with accolades, my gut started to twist in knots. I wanted to ignore the *knowing* that I was about to be cloaked with humility and hard reality. After hearing Vladimir's words, "You will be teaching the mom and tot classes, after school classes, and the exhibition teams," attempts to swallow my disappointment were futile. The weight of his words felt like a ten-ton brick fell into my lap and toppled me to the ground. How naïve I was to have believed in the charms of Vladimir when I met him two years ago!

When I left Vladimir's office after that disheartening news, I knew I had two choices: make it work or don't make it work and find another gym that would value my skills more than Vladimir. I was sorely disappointed taking stock of the past year's events. I didn't fly across the big pond to Germany for recreational gymnastic coaching. I could have done that job where I lived in Maryland.

Over the year, I watched and sopped up every bit of information about running an elite academy and coaching elite gymnasts that were afforded me. I knew that I was worthy of more than teaching the mom and tots and exhibition team. While I appreciated the value of being a good recreational and exhibition team coach, I also knew I could be a great competitive team coach. I also learned that a female coach was not welcome to become a member of the boys' club. I decided that another year could not go by with the status quo. It was time to compete with the "big boys"; I had to talk the talk and walk the walk of the big boys.

I could no longer be that girl– the nice girl – the one who was always understanding and who picked up the slack. I could no longer cover for my roommate colleagues who came into work with hangovers. I had to stop agreeing to do clerical tasks and attending to menial day-to-day scheduling business tasks. I had to definitely stop taking on the janitorial chores that Mitch and Robbie referred to as "women's work". The janitorial chores always greeted me with a wave of nausea as I couldn't escape past memories of bleaching the bathroom tile grout with a toothbrush and the annual Spring-cleaning ordeal my mother forced upon me and my siblings. She was never happy and was quick to let her opinion be known through the use of physical violence and punishment. No matter how I tried to shake the memory that played in my mind when completing janitorial chores, I couldn't.

I also knew that I couldn't be the sounding board of disgruntled parents who thought their child was *the* next Olympic star. It was clear that I was in a man's world, and I would get nowhere if I didn't start demanding more respect. Considering my ineptness in dealing with conflict and further not recognizing my ineptness, I hopped on the hope train and decided it was time to speak with Vladimir. So, with a new resolve, after swallowing my last bit of Snicker's bar, I knocked on Vladimir's office door.

"Yah, come in. What is it?" His response was unexpectedly terse, and for a second, I thought I should come back. "Nope, be strong, Isabella," I told myself, "You are playing with the big boys now." With my new self-declaration of firm resolve, I opened the door and put on my best "G'day" smile. I could see Vladimir was busy and a bit tense.

"I was wondering if we could have my annual review today instead of next week." I smiled a smile that I hoped conveyed that I was doing him a favor by conducting my review now rather than later.

"You know, Isabella, I am very happy with your work. Unfortunately, I can't today. The new coach, Stephan, is going to be starting in two days instead of next month." Vladimir spoke nonchalantly, with no consciousness of what a "new coach" meant to me!

With that news, my bubble deflated as if a dart had hit it. My hopes and dreams were in shambles, like a deflated balloon. I was shut down before I could even begin to make my case. "Oh, really? Why is he coming earlier?" One thing I learned working with Vladimir was that he was unpredictable and vague when it came to running the business. He often fired the floor exercise dance choreographers without notice, changed or canceled team meet competitions, and rarely gave me more than one day's notice when I had to travel with the exhibition team. So, hearing that Stephan was coming early was not a total shocker.

"I have agreed to train three American gymnasts who are going to the Olympic trials and need Stephan's expertise sooner than later," Vladimir shared with a tone that said, "don't question me."

"Oh, I see. So... next week, then? Okay, well right, no worries, all good." I blathered on. "So, Stephan is coming here in two days and staying where, can I ask?"

"He will only be staying at the coaches' residence with all of you for a month or so. Just until he finds an apartment." Vladimir spoke in a tone that said the issue was not up for discussion. I just stood there with no words. I didn't know if I could hold it together that minute or the next without crying. "Was there anything else, Isabella? I have got to finish this paperwork."

"Uh, no. Great chat and thanks for the info." I heard myself forcing a cheery tone to hide my disappointment. I had heard some rumblings from Mitch and Robbie about Stephan the other day at dinner, and now I understood their source of discontent. I also knew that Stephan had an article featuring him in Gymnastics Magazine. He definitely was easy on the eyes. Neither Robbie nor Mitch let on that they felt threatened by this Stephan's abilities, but I knew better. I also was well aware that neither of them wanted to share a bedroom with him either. Clearly, there was no way I was going to give up my room. I was the only girl in the house!

The next two days seemed like an eternity as I was becoming

a bit nervous about Stephan's arrival. I had seen a few photos in the Gymnast Magazine and wondered if he was as handsome in person. The sleeping arrangement was decided with a coin toss, and Robbie lost. Robbie being Robbie, took it in stride and cleared out a space for Stephan. I let Sprite know he would have to behave since we were having a fourth roommate and would be a bit more cramped!

On the afternoon of the third day, sitting in the coaches' office, my query was answered. Not only did Stephan look more handsome in person, but he seemed genuine. By the third week, our collective fears as coaches that he was going to be an egomaniac and showboat at the gym were unfounded. In fact, I was beginning to like Stephan, and it was clear that Stephan was interested in me. Each time I got within two feet of him, my knees weakened, and my heart fluttered. I often wondered if anyone noticed that I acted like a silly schoolgirl giddy with excitement after talking with Stephan. And then it happened. On the eighth week and the first evening of Stephan and I being alone at the house, he put his arms around me while I was washing Sprite's bowl and kissed me softly behind the neck. My first reaction was to freeze and overanalyze the situation. My mind was racing, questioning if he meant to kiss me or if it was an accident. Then he kissed me again.

Evidently, over the past two months, I was not fooling anyone. My lust for Stephan was not only palpable to me, but spot on, as now I was the lucky recipient of his kisses. I wanted to say "no." I wanted to reason with him and be practical. After all, it was I who made Mitch and Robbie agree to the house rules of platonic relationships only between coaches. We also agreed that none of us would bring a date back to the house. But I didn't say no. I didn't protest or remind Stephan of the house rules.

Instead, I only heard and saw in my mind's eye Queen singing the lyrics, "Don't stop me now." The more I told myself, "Stop. You can't do this. It's not right," the more I heard the lyric, "I am having a good time. Don't stop me now," resonating in my head.

I could not resist Stephan any more than a dog could resist a lemon pepper rotisserie chicken placed in front of his nose. "No," just did not feel like an option. I let Stephan's hands travel over my entire body. He skillfully touched every square inch of me. It felt as if I had fallen into a bed of freshly piled down feathers, and the soft tips massaged every pore of my skin. My body ached with pleasure with each touch. With each touch, the lyrics got louder and louder until I was completely lost to all reason. Stephan's tall, muscular six-foot-four athletic slim frame glistened with sweat as he unbuttoned my shirt and removed my laced bra. "…I feel alive… I'm floating around in ecstasy…" was playing loudly in my mind. Stephan lifted me up, and I wrapped my legs around his waist. He kicked open my bedroom door and gently tossed me on the bed. I was defenseless. His tongue reached places I did not know were possible! I squealed and screamed his name over and over with passion and delight. I succumbed to him completely – over and over again.

I woke up two hours later, lying next to Stephan. I had to pinch myself to be sure this just happened. He stirred and wrapped his arms around my waist, pulling him closer to spoon. Yup, it definitely happened. Now, the voice of reason and intellect started to kick in. I gently moved his hands and went to the kitchen to make a cuppa of English Breakfast. If ever there was a time for tea, it was now! I peeked into my room a second time to confirm the reality that he was there and gently closed the door. Stephan did not even snore! How is it possible that I had actually met my Prince Charming? Everyone insisted finding such a man was only in fairy tales. I just proved that theory incorrect! My mind was going into overdrive. How would we break the news to Mitch and Robbie? Maybe Stephan, Sprite, and I could move into a new place together. Will Vladimir fire me? Fire Stephan?

Lost in a million thoughts and scenarios, I did not hear Mitch open the front door. Startled, I jumped up and nervously started talking rapidly, "Oh, did you have a good morning? Can I make you eggs? You know Sprite missed you this evening at dinner. Do you know where Robbie is?"

Mitch looked at me with some confusion, and then the look on his face said it all. "Isabella, what's up with you? Why are you so nervous?"

"Nervous, I am not nervous. Maybe I was nervous before taking out my first eye from a corpse or driving on the Autobahn, but I am not nervous now," I retorted.

"Okay, seriously, Isabella. What gives?" he persisted.

Just at that moment, my bedroom door opened, and Stephan swaggered out, saying, "Hey bro, what's up?"

Mitch did a double-take. He looked at me, then Stephan, and then me again. My facial expression said it all. Mom D always said I wore my heart on my sleeve. "Oh no, man! I was just playing with Sprite in Isabella's room and fell asleep," Stephan quickly assured Mitch.

Mitch clearly did not buy what Stephan was selling. Mitch's instincts were that of a super sleuth. He was the James Bond and Magnum P.I. all in one. "Oh, really? That's it? You fell asleep petting Sprite?" Mitch inquired. With that, Stephan's face was that of the cat who caught the mouse. He couldn't help himself. Then, Stephan crushed me. He said the unthinkable, came over and slapped me on the bum, looked me straight in the eye, and said, "No, man. C'mon Mitch. I just tapped that. What's the big deal?"

I vaguely processed the conversation between Mitch and Stephan after that. My body felt like it had left and was looking down, watching the conversation unfold. "No, man. I, nor Robbie, tapped *that*. ", almost spitting the word "that" out vehemently. I shrunk inside myself and ran to my room. I threw myself on the bed and started to cry. I fucked up big time for sure! How could I have been so stupid? What was I thinking? I got played! What was Robbie going to think? Hell, what would Vladimir say – he couldn't find out. A few hours went by with me wallowing in sorrow in my bedroom, despite both Mitch and Stephan knocking and asking me to come out and talk. I realized I needed to pull up my big boy pants and go face them both.

I gingerly walked out of my bedroom and peered around the hallway to see if anyone was in the kitchen. To my relief, only Stephan was sitting in the dining room. "Well, Isabella, that was a bit awkward. Don't you think?"

"Awkward? You are saying that was awkward for you? What about me? How could you treat me like that?" I whispered angrily.

"Treat you like what? I know you orgasmed over and over again!

"Look, Isabella. What did you want me to say? That I am madly in love with you? Trust me, now that Mitch is sure that was a one-time thing, he won't make a big deal about it. Besides, I have been looking for an apartment and found one I am moving into next week."

Stephan's words hit my ears like the screech of cats' claws on a windowpane. I refused to hear him. I desperately wanted to pretend he never uttered the words "one-time thing." This can't be happening! In a feeble attempt to regain my pride, I tried to appear aloof and teasingly asked, "What? You are moving? So, Sprite and I can come with you?" I asked with every female charm I could muster.

Stephan looked at me like a deer in headlights. He stood stunned for a minute, turned, and walked into his bedroom. Seconds later, he came back and handed me a Colorado Springs Olympic Center sweatshirt and motioned me to put up my arms. I fell for the whole charade without missing a beat. I raised my arms while he gently put the soft white sweatshirt with the red logo of Colorado Springs over my head. Stephan zipped up the front zipper six inches from the hood. Then, he hugged me and whispered, "Hey gorgeous, you look cold. Don't worry, you will be fine. I am not a relationship guy, and you are ten years younger than me. You know work and play don't mix."

Standing there, feeling naked, I watched Stephan put his Starbuck's coffee back into the microwave. I said nothing. I did nothing. I hated myself for that. Stephan brushed by me when the microwave beeped, and he grabbed his frappa crappa whatever while I stood blindsided and in pieces. How did I do this to myself? I went back into my room, determined never to come out. I was grateful the guys all had to head out for a meet in the US and wouldn't be back for a week.

Chapter 15

True to Mom "D"'s words, the next morning came. The next morning, so did the feeling of shame and embarrassment of sleeping with Stephan. I pretended to be asleep when Mitch knocked on the door to call out that they were leaving for the airport. When Mitch knocked again, I forced myself to open the door and say good luck and went back to my bed. I didn't have to be at the gym until later, and I still had a lot to sulk about. Sprite must have known my heart was broken as he curled up inside the crook of my arm and purred. I told myself I had to get myself together. "Sprite, I can do this! I can walk in there and act like nothing has happened. Besides, I have my annual review this week and will be given a spot coaching the competitive team for sure," I reassured myself.

Over the next few weeks, I barely ate or slept. My annual review was not yet in my rearview mirror, so I still had hope of moving my career closer to my dream of coaching an Olympic gymnast. I functioned. Just functioned. I played the scene with Stephan over and over in my mind. Sometimes I was angry, and other times I found myself wet just thinking about him. It was confusing and annoying that a man I barely knew could have that much control over my thoughts. I was not going to ever let a man have power over me because of his incredible sex appeal, easy nature, and smooth-talking ever again. That was it; no man was going to control me.

A few days passed, and it was time for my annual review.

Vladimir told me earlier in the week that I could meet him at a favorite local restaurant – his treat. I parked the gym van two blocks away from the restaurant so I could practice my speech and prepare myself before going in. Vladimir greeted me with all smiles. There was no hint that he was aware of what happened at the house between Stephan and me. I was prepared to make my case and come out the victor in this review process.

We ordered a Pellegrino, a side of spetzle and brioche to start off. Vladimir started the conversation off, "Isabella, before I say anything else, I just want to thank you for your service and dedication. You have been a trooper since you started. Plus, your skill level for spotting tricks and choreographing is really blossoming."

I nodded my head and firmly stated, "Well, Vladimir, I appreciate this opportunity. I am glad you recognized that I am more than ready – overdue, actually – for moving upward and coaching elite Olympic hopefuls. When I agreed to leave everything behind and come here, I was under the impression that I would be coaching elite gymnasts – not kiddy classes and exhibition team." I felt my voice shaking a bit, but I stayed the course just as I had practiced. Proud of myself for sticking up for myself, I was ready to continue when I heard a man calling out to Vladimir.

"Vladimir! Good to see you here! How are you? Your girls are on their way to Olympics this year! No denying the talent you have at your gym," the stranger said.

I stuck my hand out assertively and said, "Hi. I am sorry, I don't know you. You are…"

The stranger shared that he was an old friend of Vladimir's. Vladimir quickly jumped in and made the introductions. "Isabella, this is Loane. Loane, this is Isabella."

"Nice to meet you, Loane." I said cheerfully. Again, Vladimir jumped in when the awkwardness was evident. "Loane, what are you doing in Germany? The Hawaiian sun isn't treating you well lately?"

"The sun always shines brightly in Hawaii." Sensing a little tension, Loane approached his next statement cautiously, "Is this beautiful young lady a new protégé of yours, Vladimir?"

I felt myself blushing at the compliment. "Not only is she my protégé, but you better watch out as she is a fierce, nationally ranked judge. Truly, a remarkable young woman," Vladimir said with a spark of pride. If this was the movie, The Exorcist, I envisioned Vladimir's head turning around in a three-sixty at that very moment.

While I appreciated the compliments, I couldn't help but think they were simply for show. One thing I learned is that appearance was everything, and gymnastics was a cutthroat business. Vladimir got up and excused himself. I was sure that was Loane's hint to disappear, but instead, Loane handed me his card, informing me he had a job opening. "Isabella, please consider coming to Hawaii. I have seen you judging at a few meets, and I can see you are an excellent technician. Don't waste your talent playing mom and tot." From the reaction on my face, it was clear that Loane knew Vladimir very well. "You know this isn't the first time I saw potential derailed," Loane added.

Vladimir returned to the table a bit annoyed. "I see you and Isabella had time to get to know each other a bit. Not to be rude, but we are in the middle of planning her next year with me. So, if you don't mind—" Vladimir's voice dropped off.

Loane gracefully took the hint and bid his farewells. As he turned, he winked. "I look forward of our next meeting and saying 'Mahalo' again."

A little flustered by his competition, Vladimir took a moment to compose himself. Putting down his glass of Pellegrino with lemon, he softly addressed me. "You are right, Isabella. I may have led you to believe that you would be working with elites right away, but that was not my intention. I know you are going to be a great elite coach – soon."

I almost choked on my pasta hearing the words "soon," which meant "not any time in the near future". My head lifted, my eyes met Vladimir's, and I knew the "not right now" was way far away. Having lost my appetite, tried to maintain a professional attitude. I could barely chew or swallow. I made myself manage my emotions. I put on my best professional smile. I didn't have the conversation I should have had. I finished, said goodbye, and returned home in the gym van.

When I pulled up to the house, it began raining, and dusk was knocking on the door. To my horror, there on the road, in front of the house, lay a ball of wet white fluff with its mouth open and blood draining from its body. It couldn't be! Not Sprite! Oh my God!

"Well, Isabella, this is what you get for being so careless with your heart," I berated myself. I jumped out of the van, numb with grief and anger. I grabbed the white Colorado Springs hoodie that I cherished from my quick tryst with Stephan and gently wrapped Sprite in it. I sat in the middle of the street, in the rain, holding Sprite on my lap, crying. I must have not seen him sneak out the door when I left. That was just the kind of irresponsible behavior I was constantly pointing out to Mitch and Robbie about, but now I was the irresponsible one. I didn't deserve love – not even from a cat. I dug a hole in the backyard of the house. I buried Sprite and made a cross out of sticks from a pine tree and sprinkled pine needles over his grave. I hung his little blue collar around the cross.

The morning sun arose, and I heard Mom "D"s voice urging me on. 'Tomorrow is always another day', she always told me. This was tomorrow. Mitch, Robbie, and Stephan would be back by lunchtime. I was ready to face life head on. I just had to regroup and work harder. I would not give up on my goals. Working for Vladimir gave me more opportunities to judge key national and international meets. It was important I didn't lose sight of that fact and used it to boost my presence as a coach.

That afternoon coaching at the gym went well, with all of us working amiably and cooperatively. Mitch and Robbie were so thrilled that two of our gymnasts made the Olympic trials in the past meet that the Stephan tryst was long forgotten. Stephan attributed the gymnasts' success to *his* last-minute routine changes; however, the three of us knew differently. The day was finally over; I was emotionally exhausted from the roller coaster ride of the past week's drama. On the way home, I shared the bad news with my roommates about Sprite's untimely demise. Their empathy and sympathy were much appreciated and helpful in making me feel like someone cared.

Because having two gymnasts making Olympic trials was as big a deal to the gymnasts as it was to the coach. To celebrate, Mitch announced he would make everyone Indian food. The kitchen started to smell like the spices of India, and the atmosphere was relaxed. I found myself smiling and laughing with a ravenous appetite. Garlic naan, chicken tikka masala, and chili paneer. Mitch went all out!

Enjoying our meal, we repaired our relationships. We toasted to the team's win and to Stephan's new apartment. While contemplating dessert, there was a faint scratching noise at the front door. Robbie heard it first and gave the "sh" finger sign.

"Did you hear that scratching?" Robbie asked.

"It's probably just that old tree branch scraping the door. I keep telling you all that branch is going to impale one of us entering the house one of these days," Mitch offered.

"Sh, sh!" Robbie said insistently. "I still hear something. I am going to check."

Robbie opened the door and yelled for me to come to the living room. "Isabella, it's a miracle!" he exclaimed.

There, in Robbie's arms, was Sprite. A little worse for the wear and obviously glad to be home. I couldn't believe my eyes. "I called the cat's name, Sprite, and Sprite turned his head!" Robbie declared, as he put Sprite down on the floor. Sprite went directly to his food bowl that I never had the heart to remove.

"It is Sprite, Isabella. Look, one green eye and one blue eye! It's official, this IS Sprite!" Mitch gleefully observed. "Oh my God, Isabella! You buried someone else's cat with a blue collar!"

"I was so distraught when I saw what I thought was my cat on the road, and further, that I thought I killed him, that I never checked his eyes! In fact, the eyes of the cat lying on the road were closed, now that I'm thinking about it." I exclaimed! I scooped up Sprite from the floor and looked at my roommates. "You know what, gentleman? This isn't a miracle. It's a sign!" With that, I proceeded to my room, rummaged through my gym bag and found Loene's business card. I began dialing his phone number confident that I would move to Hawaii where I could realize my dream. I would give Vladimir my two weeks' notice. I was moving onward and forward! Tomorrow was another day!

Chapter 16

I woke up with Sprite with a revived spirit. The phone call to Loene was exhilarating the night before. He did not seem surprised that I called. We talked for an hour and I emphasized that I would not make another move unless I was guaranteed a competitive team coaching spot. I also negotiated a higher salary and free room and board in a one-bedroom apartment on the beach. All that was left, was to tell Vladimir. I skipped out the door and jumped in the car with Robbie. I was moving forward and nearer to my dream.

Vladimir was in his office and I thought it best to share my news sooner than later. We had a half hour before the first recreational group came in the gym. I knocked on Vladimr's door, but did not wait for him to say come in. He looked up from the phone and motioned for me to sit. My palms were a little sweaty and my stomach wretched with nerves. Every second seemed endless and I just wanted to get out my resolve to Vladimir.

Vladmir hung up the phone and tuned to me. "What can I do for you, Isabella?"

"Hear me out." I said with a bit of inflection.

"Are you going to ask me something or tell me something?" he inquired with a hint of audible stress.

I took a deep breath and attacked delivering the news like a man – direct and to the point. "I am giving you my two week notice. I came here with the understanding that I would be competitive team coach. I have another offer and am going to take it."

My words got Vladimir's attention. At first, he tried to dissuade me from leaving by offering me $50 extra a month and four less hours of teaching recreational gymnasts. My insistence that I teach competitive team was met with resistance and to no avail. The recreational gymnasts were filing in the lobby and Vladimir and I made no progress in negotiating. I had clarity that I must go to Hawaii.

"Look, Vladimir, I really, really appreciate everything you did for me, but it's time for me to go. I know that, and you know that. Unless you offer me a competitive team coaching position, I just can't stay. I will be leaving in two weeks."

I turned to walk away and Valdimir piped up, "Can you give me three weeks? I feel like you owe me that much. Don't you?"

Despite my anxiousness to leave, Vladimir managed to make me feel guilty so I agreed to three weeks. "Oahu, here I come," I told myself as I bounded out of the office onto the gym floor to start my group on the uneven bars.

For the next two weeks, days went by without a hitch. Wake up, work out, coach, go to happy hour, dance and start it all again the next day. At the start of third week with Vladimir's gym, Sprite began to sense something would change as he watched me start packing the few things I acquired over the past year. At the end of the third week, two days before leaving, Mitch and Robbie surprised me by taking me to my favorite Spetzel house. When we got to the restaurant, Stephan was already there.

"Stephan, I am surprised that you came even though we still coach together. It's been a bit weird seeing you at the gym this past week. You know the way we left things before you moved out wasn't exactly settling." I managed to say.

"Now, now Isabella, it doesn't have to be like that. Let's just accept that you had a different agenda than I did when we met."

It infuriated me that Stephan didn't even blink when he delivered his line with confident swagger. It infuriated me even more that I cared what he was saying.

"Different agendas? Next time it would behoove you to let the girl know the only agenda you have is your agenda of get in, get out." I said feeling satisfied I stuck up for myself.

"Well Isabella, let's not get snarky with each other. After all, this is a good bye dinner. You are the one running, not me." Stephan retorted.

"First of all, Stephan, I am not running anywhere. Vladimir hasn't upheld his end of the deal. I expected to be coaching competitive team and he didn't come through. Oh, that's right – he brought you in to coach competitive team. I am moving toward my goals and dreams." I boldly announced.

"Seriously, Isabella. Get over yourself. You may be a cute little Aussie girl with a few skills, but you are not the next Bella Karoly." Stephan was getting ready to give another Stephan-ism when Mitch jumped in to assist the two of us boxing like kangaroos.

"Ouch!" Mitch tried to lighten the mood. "Our table is ready, shall we?"

"Thank you, Mitch. Yes, we should all put the past in the past and enjoy a yummy dinner. Afterall, this is a celebratory good bye gathering, is it not? " I replied while following the hostess.

The hostess seated us at a booth in the back. I wasn't sure if it was because we were casually dressed or because of the slightly loud row she may have over heard while we were waiting in the lobby.

With a glass of wine each in hand, Stephan raised to toast, "Bygones!"

We all cheered, "Bygones!"

"Of course, we don't want to see you go, Isabella." Robbie said endearingly.

"You are such a suck, Robbie," I blushed.

Stephan wasn't having it. You could tell he was uncomfortable with where the conversation was headed. He quickly changed the subject. "So, Isabella, what was one of your favorite memories from living with these two jack offs this year?"

"Oh, matey, I have so many." I said with a sexy tone. "Where should I start? With the stale smelly sweat odor that pervaded the room when I first came to the house, or the continuous stream of dirty boxers lining the hallway?"

Everyone laughed. "C'mon, Isabella. We could not have been that bad! Were we?"

"No, I can forgive you both for being wankers because you both loved Sprite! Except you – Stephan. I think you were faking being an animal lover just so I would succumb to your effervescent charms." I couldn't resist one last jab.

"Now, see Isabella, that's where you are wrong, right Stephan? I know for a fact you are not a cat lover, but a dog lover!" Mitch teased.

"Okay, Mitch! You got me. You called me out." Stephan sounded a bit uncomfortable. "Yes, Isabella, I confess. I am not a cat lover, but I do happen to love dogs and horses."

Robbie raised his glass, "I'm so glad we got that critical bit of information cleared up! Now, in all seriousness, there has to be something you are going to miss when you leave us here alone in the cold, snowy streets of Stuttgart!"

"Well, I have definitely taken a liking to Nutella, but still miss my Vegemite." I offered.

"Good, good – I see you have good taste with Nutella." Mitch exclaimed.

"Actually, Mitch, I loved quite a few things while I have been here. I really enjoyed the flammkuchen with Nutella that I ate at the Christmas Markets. Germany definitely has the market on the Christmas Market. So many cool things to see, great street performers – especially the angel costumes – and the lights!" I reminisced with a smile.

"I agree with you, Isabella. The Christmas scene here is unbelievably fun!" Mitch added.

"When I first met you, I thought you were going to be a sushi, sashimi type of guy. I honestly don't believe you have one spec of Asian in you!" I said laughingly.

"Here, here! I have been saying the exact same thing for the past few years! I was so excited when I found out I was going to have an Asian roommate. I pictured nights of enjoying homemade noodles and freshly made sushi, but instead it's been all fried chicken and steaks. Even though I am Italian, I didn't expect to be cooking pasta for Mitch!" Randy explained.

"How ghastly! We have shown our true stereotype-colors! We all know you are full of it Robbie. I don't know how the two of you have survived, as my observation is that neither you nor Mitch eat anything but Mahi, Indian food and leftover take out." I teased.

We sat exchanging banter for the next hour.

"It's getting late. I am going to need a box. Anyone else?" Robbie asked while motioning for the server to bring the bill.

"Here you go Isabella, pay up." Robbie exclaimed while handing me the dinner check.

"Ha, ha. Don't have to be a knob up to my last minute in

Germany!" I tossed the bill back to Stephan.

"You know I was just messing with you, Isabella. C'mon, admit it, it was funny." Stephan chided.

The bill was split among the three men. I felt good about how I was leaving Germany. Admittedly, I was still a little raw emotionally from Stephan's shenanigans, but I was ready to move forward.

It was a gorgeous Spring-like day in Germany the day Sprite and I boarded the plane to reach our new destination, Oahu, Hawaii. I had no idea what to expect. Of course, I knew of the stereotypes of hula skirts, fresh flower leis, Hawaiian native music and pineapple growers. I had never considered Hawaii to be the center of the international gymnastic scene, although when thinking about the climate in Hawaii, it did make perfect sense. Gymnasts flourish more in warm, tropical environments since they don't have to battle significant muscular temperature changes when practicing or competing.

Filing past the first and executive class sections on the plane, Sprite and I settled in window in economy seat 36F. We were lucky to have a window seat in a two seat aisle so the twenty one hour flight, with two plane changes, would be bearable with a coach ticket. Sprite's carrier had to be placed under the seat in front of me, so leg room was a bit cramped; otherwise, all was looking up! The flight was full. I made a mental note to let Scottie know he was correct! Judging by the passengers, people *did* seem to save their whole lives to have a holiday in Hawaii!

After my initial flight took off, I realized I was going from one mountainous area to another. I was not nervous. I had done this before – took risks moving on. During the second leg of my flight, I thought about all the challenges I had faced. I patted myself on the back as I was still standing. No, not just standing –

I was thriving. I felt hopeful and knew this was my shot. I also told myself that no matter how handsome or charming a man may be that I may meet in the future, I am not going to fall for his charms. I was not going to be hurt again.

Sprite and I went from airport to airport to airport with little stress. I was fortunate that Sprite adapted to any situation in which he was placed. His pure white coat and two differently colored eyes also got him pets wherever we went. Finally, we boarded the last plane bound for Oahu. I was told I had a car waiting, and this time I had confirmed that Sprite would not be denied access to the car before arranging my pick-up. As the plane began its descent, the mountains encircled my eye's view. Close to landing, I could see the lush, green foliage and beautiful plants that lined the mountains and area below. This felt more like home. I couldn't wait to get settled and get to the beach! "Surf's up," I thought!

Once I and Sprite cleared customs and retrieved the luggage, I managed to stay awake to soak in the pleasant scenery to my new home. I believed that luck didn't just fall in one's lap, but that luck was recognizing opportunity. I had looked and took this opportunity when it presented itself and was excited. This opportunity was going to move my career to another stratosphere toward elite level coaching status. Luggage gathered and admitted by customs I was in the transportation area of the airport searching for my name. As if it were Deja Vue, I spotted a man in shorts and a blue and pink floral short sleeved button down shirt holding the sign, "Notski". I thought to myself that the good news was Hawaiians spoke English so the communication was much simpler than my arrival in Germany.

To my surprise, the driver greeted me with a beautiful lei of aromatic white, pink-tipped, ginger flowers. The small, potent flower was intoxicating. Sprite seemingly loved the lei as well, as he kept butting his head against the flowers and smelling them.

"Yes!", I thought, "This is the right move for Sprite and I!" I was already in love with Hawaii and had not even seen my apartment nor stepped into the gymnastic facility. The driver pulled up in front of my apartment. I was promised a one bedroom apartment on the beach, and while I was slightly disappointed, I still felt my lodging was better than expected. Afterall, deep down I knew I was probably not *actually* going to get a beach front apartment. What I did get was a small studio apartment about a half mile from the beach facing the direction of the beach. Being a bit more experienced with contract negotiations than when negotiating with Vladimir, I never expected to get everything from Leone that I asked for; however, this was a good start. Perhaps the next time, I would have to be even more specific when negotiating.

The studio apartment Sprite and I occupied was on the second floor. I didn't mind as I was sure to get a little warm up and warm down exercise walking up and steps on a daily basis. I quickly learned that I lived only three blocks from the main freeway known as "the Pali". The Pali connected the wayward islands to Honolulu. The gym facility was easily accessible by public bus transportation as the gym was "down the Pali" per the local jargon. Exploring my neighborhood, I learned that kayak rentals were plentiful. I hoped I could fit kayaking in my budget.

Before leaving Germany, I contacted Jan and let him know to sell my car. I insisted he take a third of the sale price, but Jan being Jan – refused. I hated to give up my Mustang, but I realized it was not of any use to me in Hawaii as traffic was notoriously bad, parking expensive and shipping my car there even more expensive. On the bright side, the sale of the Ghia afforded me enough money to buy a cat condo for Sprite, keep food in the refrigerator, possibly kayak and find a yoga class. Overall, having a few dollars convinced me that I was living the life!

I arrived in Hawaii earlier than was necessary. I had two days before I had to start working for Leone's and going to the gymnastic facility. I wrote a list of "must do's". Firstly, the apartment received the morning sun, so purchasing black-out blinds was a must if I was going to be able to sleep. Sleep for a gymnastics coach is similar to that of restaurant workers working the dinner shift. I didn't start coaching until two p.m. or three p.m. and did not return home until nine thirty or ten p.m. It was an unspoken understanding amongst coaches that going straight home from work and falling asleep was highly improbable. The body and mind was simply too jazzed to calm down and sleep. Typically, I fell asleep between one a.m. and two a.m., so I was not good at rising early. The purchase of the black-out blinds allowed me to sleep in comfortably.

My second day as a resident of Oahu hit me as my new reality. Today was my first day working for Leone. I found my nerves were bubbling a bit inside. "Natural reaction," I told myself.

Walking out of the apartment, it was a perfect sunny day with a slight breeze. I had time to go get a smoothie from a shop adjacent to the bus stop before catching the bus to ride down the Pali. Mom "D"'s calming words of "Nerves are good for you" came to mind and helped me feel more at ease sitting on the bus going down the Pali.

On the bus ride, I calculated my ability to afford a gym membership so I could take yoga to keep my muscles pliable and renting a kayak. I felt I would be able to do both. This was a great start I thought and promised myself I would seek out yoga classes and cheap kayak rentals soon. The bus stop was one block from the gymnastics center. It took precisely twenty five minutes. I gleefully jumped off the bus and walked to the front door of the gym. "Here we go." I thought, and with that I swallowed one last gulp of nervous courage and opened the door.

My first impression entering the gym facility was much different than that of Vladimir's gym. I was one of two women coaches employed. I knew from experience the male coaches would be watching my every move the first few weeks wondering if I was capable of coaching at a competitive level. Walking into the facility, Leone called out.

"Maholo, Ms. Notski." Leone called out from the second story office. "Come on up and join me!"

There, I was greeted with a lei by two of the male coaches currently working. I thought I was in heaven. I also could have never imagined several leis circling my neck could feel heavy! The scents were intoxicating. After the quick meet and greet, Leone provided me with the lay of the land. Leone had a separate office from staff. He provided a comfortable office for staff which included up-to-date technology – internet access. My gut told me I was in the right place. I was moving up in the world!

Leone broke the quiet, "To introduce you to all the staff, there will be a welcome luncheon at a local's favorite restaurant tomorrow. Sound good?" Leone asked

"Wow! That's not necessary, but yes, yes, I would love that." I replied.

"Today, you will shadow Kalani and Patrick coaching compulsory level team and optional level three teams. Tomorrow you will begin coaching level three team compulsory on beam and optional routines on floor exercise. See – I keep my promise to you." Leone winked and smiled.

After listening to Leone, while I was grateful for being assigned coaching the lower level three compulsory and optional teams, I thought I should mention my desire to teach level five or six optional gymnasts. My gut told me otherwise. I quickly checked myself and did not ask. I was getting better at listening to my gut – I hoped.

The gym had a good flow relative to how gymnasts moved from one apparatus to the next. The fear of gymnasts colliding was at a minimum. I appreciated that safety factor which was not the case at Vladmir's facility. The girls I would coach were well trained and disciplined in the sport. They welcomed me with open arms the first day of arrival. It felt good to be there.

I and Sprite settled into our Hawaiian work routine quickly. I found my solace and strength in my daily routine of kayaking, yoga class, smoothies and catching the bus to head to coach. I was very fortunate that one of the coaches owned several kayaks and brought one to the apartment for me to use. Every morning, I would put on sunscreen before I did anything else. Being an Aussie, the familiar public service announcement jingle, "Slip, Slop and Slap", was forever burned in my brain. Slip was for slipping on a long sleeve sun shirt. Slop meant put on sunscreen. and slap meant wear a hat! The little jingle was short and sweet and one I sung every morning in Hawaii. I would then proceed to use tie down straps to secure the kayak on the trolley and walk it the half mile to the beach.

Living at the northern end of Kailua, I was blessed with the opportunity to kayak with numerous sea turtles that made their home about 800 feet from the shore line. I got to know the sea turtles well by physical markings and their personalities. I named one Scratchy due to the many scratches on his shell. Another, I dubbed Bully for obvious reasons. My favorite was Crackers, as this sea turtle was funny. Crackers would come up to my kayak, poke his head out of the water and turn a bit on his side and continue swimming. Crackers made me laugh every day. I wondered if he had a neurological balance or shell weight problem. Crackers looked healthy and was well liked by the others, but was more playful and curious than Bully or Scratchy. When I reached a tiny island about 1 mile off shore, I would beach the kayak and snorkel a bit. The array of brightly colored fish was amazing! I felt like all the sea life were my family. I felt truly connected to the ocean creatures. Every day I went to coach, the team girls would ask me which of the sea turtles I saw. They would giggle and gave me the nickname Turtle Whisperer.

I didn't mind having another nickname after God's creatures, especially the magnificent sea turtle. No one on the Island knew me to be Pladdy or Platypuss. Turtle Whisperer felt right and suited me. In many ways, I was like a turtle. I kept a lot of emotional pain inside the shell of a body and, at times, was a bit timid to poke my head and test the waters with those around me. While I may have been willing to take risks in life, I did so blindly because I followed my heart. I could quickly adapt to new situations and people around me because I kept my feelings to myself. I was no "Pollyanna", but I always presented as cheery and emotionally strong. I never digested negative emotional situations but brushed them off like a piece of lint that landed on a black coat. Once I brushed off the lint, my outside shell appeared perfect. That tiny piece of lint went drifting away nowhere to be found and could not inconvenience another.

While I enjoyed living in paradise, there was a down side to my situation. Living in Hawaii was expensive. The sale of the Ghia did not go as far as I would have hoped. My salary, while better than that in Germany, also did not go as far as I hoped. In mentioning to Coach Jimmie how expensive it was for food, he was shocked that I was even buying food. Unbeknown to me, Hawaii Happy Hour offered fresh Mahi and other seared or blackened fish tacos and was a regular stop off for the male coaches three to five times a week. How they could have forgotten to entrust me with such important information was beyond me! For almost two months I was stretching my budget and living basically on one smoothie and macaroni and cheese on a daily basis. I had to pay utilities and bus fees and that typically tapped me out each month financially. The money from the car sale was long gone as I had to pay Sprite's vet fees and I had a few doctor appointments here and there.

After Jimmie told me the coaches Happy Hour strategy for eating free, but healthy, food, I was ecstatic. I also found out that with happy hour came music. Every Monday, Wednesday and Friday, after coaching, I and my two colleagues went to Happy Hours and ate and danced. I loved to dance. I had become a dancing fool. I had rhythm and easily found dancing partners. I would meet attractive, energetic, tall men – but always reminded myself that I was there to coach, not to get into a relationship. Staying focused on a goal does not allow for the distraction of relationships.

My favorite Happy Hour spot was the Pookie. One thing Hawaiians loved was karaoke. At the Pookie, a regular came in and displayed, what he thought, was spectacular dancing and singing skills. He was about 5'4" and wore a shirt that had bold black lettering "Speed Dancer". The locals at the bar informed me that Speed Dancer invented this name for himself. Indeed, watching his speed dancing was amazing entertainment. His dancing moves could be described as Michael Jackson's Moonwalk meets Formula one combined with kickboxing. He always wore a white-yellow mesh shirt with jeans. I could never decide if he was emulating John Travolta's disco days or one of the Village People. At any rate, his super fast dancing required that most patrons clear the floor to avoid a dancing collision. And *that* is how I met my future.

While exiting the floor for Speed Dancer, I bumped into a few very sweet Canadian hockey players. While three out of the five were in a drunken, incoherent stupor, two of the players were quite charming and funny. The funniest of the bunch was named Terry. He was kind, understanding and handsome. He, unlike the others had a bit of rock and roll soul and was an excellent dancer. Unfortunately, he was also married. Just my luck. During our conversations, he kept telling me that his best mate, Grant, would be perfect for me. I just giggled and replied, If I had a dollar for every time a friend told me they had my perfect mate, I would be rich. But something about this very sincere, baby faced, Canadian hockey player made me believe there could be a possible man living out there like him. It gave me hope. Of course, I reminded myself I was just a few weeks shy of one year working with Leone and no one would change my destiny of greatness. The night turned into the early morning and I left the Canadians to get some much needed sleep. The rigorous coaching schedule and gymnastic attendance was all consuming.

The next morning, I woke up refreshed and prepared for my routine of kayaking, yoga, smoothie and coaching. However, I had a few extra dollars and decided that instead of a smoothie, it was time to treat myself to a burger and fries at Burger King. I figured I was eating so much free mahi, that one hamburger and a few fries were something I could afford financially. I also felt that I could afford the calories and crappy nutritional level every now and then. So after yoga, I walked down the street past a typical one story Hale Halawai – a traditional Hawaiian building boasting of open walls on at least one side to achieve fantastic air flow – and rounded the corner to the Burger King. My decision to treat myself started to play on my mind.

Waiting my turn at the one Burger King on the Westward side of the Island, I thought about the romance the Hale Halawai architecture elicited in my mind. The server broke me from my thought,

"Welcome to Burger King. What can I help you with?" he asked with a look that said he really wasn't interested or paying attention.

So, I ordered a medium Diet Coke. Evidently, the server did not understand my accent as the server kept telling me they didn't have "cake".

To my surprise, a deep voice behind me said, "I think she means the drink – Coke. Not the cake dessert." I whipped my head around ready to say thank you to a stranger and go on about my day. This thank you should have been a five second exchange; however, this man was tall, clearly an athlete, with the brightest white smile – minus one front tooth. I never watched hockey so at the time I had no idea that a missing front tooth was rather common when hockey players get "high-sticked" in the mouth during games.

Instead of a five second exchange, I sputtered and stammered my words of thanks for several minutes. Babbling away, I could feel the sexual tension between the two of us. While waiting for my burger and Diet Coke, I felt this man's smile searing directly through me as he stood behind me, On my way out, I felt a tap on my shoulder,

"My name is Grant. Can I take you out tonight?"

I thought this could be a coincidence, but I asked anyway.

"By any chance you wouldn't be the Grant who is friends with a Terry, would you?"

Grant answered swiftly and confidently, "Yes mam! How do you know Terry?"

"Well, he was the only sober, coherent one at the Pokie Bar and Grill last night. I guess Canadian hockey players can throw back tinnies like the swizzies I know back home in Australia," I laughed.

"Are you speaking English, because I have no idea what a *tinnie* or a swizzy *is*." Grant replied flashing the beaming smile minus one upper tooth.

"Oh! Tinnies are beers and a swizzy is one who drinks too many and acts stupid," I informed Grant.

'Well, now I really want to get to know you. The guys and I were just in Melbourne, Australia. Are you from around there?" Grant asked followed by a dazzling smile.

"Nope. I'm from the other side of the continent – West Australia. That's cool you have been to Australia matey." I smiled hoping to encourage the conversation to continue.

"So, miss?" his voice dropped off.

"Isabella. My name is Isabella." I quickly interjected.

"Okay Miss Isabella. What time am I picking you up and where?" he asked insistently.

"Hmmm. You are a bold one now! I am not sure I said yes yet. In fact, I am waiting for a proper date request. Exactly what type of girl do you think I am?" I teased.

"Oh, that's how it is." Grant smiled showing his missing tooth and dimples. "So, very beautiful lady, would you give me the pleasure of dining with you tonight?"

Grant was not only charming but built like a brick house. It was easy to see he had an easy demeanor and a sense of humor. I knew I was smitten and was not great at playing hard to get.

I replied with my best cheeky tone, "So will you be bringing Terry or is this a big boy date?"

"I could bring Terry; however, I think you would tire of his never ending resume of credentials and his accomplishments. I am just a simple Yukon man so I think it should just be the two of us." Grant confidently replied.

Just when I was about to answer, Terry came walking in the Burger King wondering what was taking so long.

"Grant, I thought you were making the burgers! What in the hell..." seeing me, Terry's voice trailed off.

"Well, I'll be a monkey's Uncle. If it isn't Miss Pokie dancer! Barbie, right?" he smiled.

"Not even close! But good try. Was that supposed to be an Aussie funny?" I quipped.

"It was a good guess, don't you think?" Terry smirked.

"Well, only because your mate, Grant, is such a gentleman, I won't make you guess my name. My name is Isabella, and it is nice to run into you again. I was just explaining to Grant how you and I met! Speed dancer man was a crack up!" I explained watching Grant's reaction keenly.

I could see Grant was getting nervous. Perhaps it was a competitive thing between mates to so I gave Grant a flirty wink.

"So, about tonight. You can pick me up at Leone's Gymnastics Academy. It is directly next to the American Red Cross building on the corner of Bayla and Hani. I won't be done coaching until nine p.m." I stammered a little too quickly hoping he didn't see how anxious I was to have a date with him.

Grant's face lit up, "Okay, little Sheila! I will be there nine p.m. sharp."

"I need to get going, I am going to miss my bus! Oh – and

my name's not Sheila." I answered lightly.

"What? You have to take a bus?" Terry inquired.

"Yes, I didn't ship my car over when I moved here." I replied secretly hoping for a ride.

Punching Grant's shoulder, Terry quickly got Grant's hint and volunteered taking me to work. "C'mon. We don't bite and you two can get to know each other better!"

"Okay, you are quite the salesman, Terry. Well, Grant, I need to sit in the front as I easily get car sick. Hope you are good with that." I beamed.

Grant and Terry grabbed their burgers and fries and we loaded in the rental vehicle. My mind was reeling with thoughts of disbelief. I pinched myself to remind myself that I was NOT, under any circumstances, NOT going to be taken in by this handsome, athletic, kind, brown-eyed sexy specimen of a hockey player. Nope – I was on a mission to make it to the Olympics as a coach and nothing was going to stop me!

The silence in the car was awkward at first and broken by Grant. "That's great you coach gymnastics. My niece is taking gymnastics. She will be excited to hear that I met a bonified national coach working with Olympic hopefuls."

"Awww, that's sweet you have a niece. I have been coaching for some time. I coach competitive gymnasts and want to become an Olympian coach." I declared.

It was clear that Terry and Grant were good friends based on their banter. Both bragged about the others' accomplishments. Grant couldn't say enough about Terry's leadership of the Canadian National Games, and Terry couldn't' brag enough about Grant's hockey skills and gold mining knowledge. Two blocks from the gym I changed the conversation to the details of my impending date.

"Since you have been visiting Hawaii, have you found a favorite place for our date? I get off at nine p.m." I inquired.

"I was leaving that up to you, Isabella. I will be back here at nine p.m. Ladies choice." Grant quickly offered.

"Oh, you know how to charm a woman." Speaking with Grant was fun and easy. The flow, minus Terry's interruptions, was titillating. My instincts told me Grant and I were going to get along well.

"Terry, here's my stop. Pull over to the right. I am still the newbie and I am already running late by five minutes!" I jumped out of the car, skipped up the steps, opened the gym door and waved goodbye. Luckily, no one seemed to notice that I was five minutes tardy. The day seemed to drag on and on. At 8:45, I saw Grant shyly enter the gym and I waved. I put up my index finger to show I needed a minute. I watched Leone walk over to Grant. It was apparent Grant and Leone were engaged in a sports discussion based on the hockey swing motion Leone was showing Grant.

"Okay, girls! We will see you tomorrow. Time to wrap it up! Stay loose and focused during your cool down." I said trying to hide my excitement that Grant was there.

Waving to Grant while approaching he and Leone, I could not stop smiling.

"Grant was telling me he is a semi-pro hockey player. I love hockey! Grant is welcome here anytime." Leone smiled and gave me the nod.

"Oh, who would have guessed. Well, if you two gentlemen are done jabber jawing about hockey, this lady is ready for her date!" I teased.

Outside of the gym, Grant was a gentleman. He opened the car door in his aqua blue stylish Tommy Bahama shirt with cleanly pressed khakis. So far, so good, I thought.

"Where to, my lady?" Grant asked smiling.

"We are going to the Why Knot restaurant. They are on the water and will have a live band. Just get off the Pali at Naila Street. "I confidently stated.

Throughout dinner, Grant seemed easy going. He and I easily fell into comfortable banter and conversation. I learned he was from Northwest Territory, Canada and had several brothers and sisters. He told corny jokes, had a sheepish smile, and eyes that sparkled when he spoke. Dinner went smoothly and we found we shared many food dislikes. This was very important, especially since I didn't cook. We also quickly learned we came from dysfunctional families. Dinner over and plates cleared, to ensure our date continued, I knew I had to make a good suggestion.

"Dinner was lovely. Let's hit the bar and see what band is playing." I suggested.

"Sure, but I must warn you I am not a great dancer." Grant took my hand and led the way.

"It's okay, you are easy on the eyes and your smile is infectious-even with a missing tooth." I replied

Entering the bar room, we both looked in horror as the stage was clearly set for karaoke! "I should have known. Hawaii is the karaoke global capital, I think. So I will, if you will!" I encouraged Grant.

We both laughed uncontrollably – of course, the few glasses of wine at dinner lightened the mood! The tourists and Asian residents loved karaoke and were ripping it up on stage. Suddenly, I heard the M.C. say, "Next up is Isabella singing White Wedding! Come up to the stage, Isabella."

The look on Grant's face was priceless! "You did not, you

knob! I can't sing, Grant!" I adamantly explained.

"Now is your time to shine sexy Sheila. Go on up." With that, Grant gently took my hand, kissed it, and gestured "Your fans await."

Not wanting to disappoint and having several glasses of liquid courage, I decided to participate. Awkwardly, I walked up on stage, grabbed the microphone and belted out the words to White Wedding. I danced and pranced, and flirted with Grant from the stage. I got a few whistles and claps of approval as I left the stage. We sang and danced and drank until well after midnight. Grant leaned in and whispered in my ear.

"That was... what can I say? That was..." Without finishing, Grant touched my hair and then my face. He lifted my chin and sensually kissed my lips. Electricity ran through my body in a rush. I was hooked and knew I could not resist.

"Let's get out of here and walk on the beach!" I quickly sputtered after inhaling Grant's kiss.

I grabbed his hand and we ran out onto the white sandy beach. Grant pulled my waist to his and kissed me with incredible fervor. His kisses shot through my body as my mind screamed for more. The moon's light flickering on the sand mimicked the dancing, twinkling stars above. Sitting on the beach with Grant was magical. I didn't want the night to end. His touch, smell, gleaming eyes and smile were captivating. My internal battle was going to be a rough one. Grant versus my goals. I would have to keep my resolve. While lost in the magical moment, I heard a faint scratching noise.

"Sh! What is that?" I whispered.

Grant and I strained our eyes looking for the source of the sound. "Look! It's a turtle coming up!" I shrieked a little too loudly while jumping up and down.

"Yes, it is, little lady! Would you look at that?" Grant whispered watching the large, sea turtle laboriously pushing the sand from its strong clawed feet toward us.

The minutes seemed like hours before the majestic sea turtle completed making its birthing bed and began laying eggs. We were watching a miracle at its finest. Both Grant and I were mesmerized with joy. Finally, Grant broke the silence.

"Well, Isabella, I don't want to leave but I have to get back. Terry and I are getting up at six a.m. for a seven a.m. tee time on the North side of the island.

Grant stood up, handed me his strong grip and I leapt to my feet. The silence in the car back to my home was easy and fulfilling sitting next to Grant. Without speaking, we both understood the totality of the evening. Pulling up to my apartment, Grant got out of the car and opened my car door. Of course, I was impressed.

"Wow, Grant. Opening doors can get you places!" I laughed teasingly.

"I hope so." Grant replied. My eyes searched his until he leaned down, lifted my chin and kissed me gently on the lips. "So, shall we repeat this tomorrow?"

"Absolutely! I sure hope the animal gods bless us again!" I managed to say as I turned to go in the apartment and turned back to blow a kiss when I opened the door.

Grant watched me close the door standing in front of the driver's side door.

"I am going to marry you one day, Isabella!" Grant suddenly yelled across the driveway.

Not able to resist, I retorted, "Catch me if you can. See you tomorrow. Same time, same place."

Chapter 17

Grant came the next day to the gym after practice, and we had another lovely dinner. The attraction was undeniable. The sexual tension was also undeniable. Grant was funny. He also had a very simple black-and-white view of the world. I was all about the grey and in between. He loved animals as much as I did. When Grant spoke of his hometown and the muskox, bear, porcupine, and moose, his respect and love for nature ran deep through his soul. For a week, Grant and I danced, ate, laughed, kissed, shared stories, and got to know each other. His last weekend was coming up. Fortunately, I had no competitive meets I had to attend on his last weekend.

To my surprise, Grant asked if I would like to come and stay with him at a five-star resort on the east side of the island, Turtle Bay. I wanted to jump up and down and say Yes! through a megaphone, but I played it cool and told him I had to check my schedule. My friends at college taught me that if you want a man, acting indifferent is a sure-fire way to get and maintain his interest. I wanted this man! I was not a game player and knew that I wore my heart on my sleeve. So... I clapped and enthusiastically said, "Yes!"

So much for remaining cool and indifferent, I thought. The day before Grant and Terry had to go back to the Yukon, Grant came to my apartment and picked me up. The drive around the island took less than two hours. We were both in awe of the beauty of the lush, green mountains and various waterfalls.

When we arrived at Turtle Bay, we were greeted with traditional leis and shown to our suite. Grant had arranged for champagne and chocolate-covered strawberries! It was beautiful!

My first reaction was such glee that I jumped on the bed as if it were a trampoline. It felt freeing!

"That's my Izzy! Do I need to give you the nickname Dizzy Izzy?" Grant's face lit up, watching me like that of a child amazed seeing the NYC Rockefeller Christmas tree light up in all its wonder.

"I see, now I'm Izzy – I like it! Why don't you join me? We can be two monkeys jumping on the bed!" I giggled.

"Let's hit the links!"

My look of confusion said it all. "The links?"

"The golf course! I rented golf clubs for you," he informed me, beaming.

I couldn't wait to see him in action. I also couldn't wait to show off my athletic expertise. Little did I know the challenge of golf would humble and ground me.

Settled in the golf cart, we pulled up to the first tee box. Grant confidently stepped up, gripped the club with confidence, brought the club head behind his shoulder, and let it drop. The ping of the ball and club connecting was almost as mesmerizing as Grant's superior physique. His well-molded biceps, exquisite six-pack, perfect waist, and strong legs had me captivated. Lost in lust, Grant handed me a 3-iron and said, "You're up, Izzy. Seeing as you are a virgin golfer, how about I come behind you and guide the club?"

"There is nothing I would like more – to help, I mean – with hitting the ball," I uttered cheerfully while giving him my best sexy wink and smile. "Hey, wait a minute! Why don't I get the big head like you used?"

"I don't think you can handle the big club just yet! You have to start slowly!" Grant assured me.

"Oh, I see. I'll look forward to hitting with the bigger clubs… later."

"Okay, Izzy, get serious."

Grant came up behind me and helped me grasp the 3-iron. His body heat was intoxicating. With all my confidence, I gripped the club, kept my eye on the ball, and let the club drop! With a ping, I watched the ball go about eighty yards.

"I know mine didn't fly to the moon like yours but not a bad start. I am ready to hit again by myself." With that proclamation, I took another golf ball, placed it on the tee, readied my stance, and confidently let the club swoop down and connect. I watched the ball go approximately a hundred yards in the air and fall two yards from my feet.

Roaring with laughter, I looked at Grant. "Okay, so that was not what I expected." Neither Grant nor I could stop laughing. With that, he grabbed me by the waist, pulled me to his lips, and sweetly whispered, "Later."

The golf outing got better with each tee. Grant was an amazing athlete. He was an amazing kisser. He was, well, amazing!

Golf completed, my ego only slightly bruised, Grant and I had a romantic dinner. Everything about Grant exuded sex and sex appeal. We watched the sunset together. I wanted the evening to stand still in time. It was perfect. He was perfect.

"I am knackered, and tomorrow you are leaving. I will miss you, Grant. I know that's stupid as we just met," I stammered, hoping not to jinx the evening.

"Now Izzy, I am going to talk to you every day. We are going to figure this out! I am going to find a job for you, and you can move to the Yukon!" Grant volunteered.

"Seriously! Yeah right, as if that's going to happen. One day at a time is probably best, but right now I am ready for bed."

With that, Grant and I cuddled in bed and started talking about sports, pets, dreams, and gold mining. I learned he owned a trucking company with his brothers and wanted to be either a pro golfer or a gold miner. He learned that I wanted to be an international elite gymnastics coach and coach in a summer Olympics. Then the hard part came – sleeping! Neither I nor Grant could sleep as the sexual tension grew to be almost unbearable. With firm resolve, I managed to fall asleep for a few hours. I woke up to ocean waves, English Breakfast tea, and Grant's kisses.

We were both silent most of the way back. While I was elated to be near Grant, I dreaded his leaving! It was as if I was afraid to speak as I thought I may lose precious memories. Pulling into the apartment parking lot, I looked at Grant with a look that said, "Don't go," and he looked back with a look that said, "I don't want to go."

"You know I don't want to leave you, Izzy. I am going to call you every day. I promise."

"Promises, promises. I have heard that before. But I am willing to give it a chance." With those words, Grant grabbed me by the waist and pulled me toward his body. There was only one thing I knew – I wanted this man in my life. His kisses were magical and made me feel as if I was the only person in the world who existed. The next day seemed a bit surreal. I went through the motions of working but had no desire to eat free Mahi or watch "speed dancer," or hang with the coaches. I only wanted to hear from Grant. I wanted him to show up at the gym, sweep me off my feet, and whisper sweet nothings in my ear. After my daily routine – kayaking, working out, smoothie, and bus down the Pali – I went home and waited. I waited until four a.m. and fell asleep.

Waking up the next morning, I realized I had not yet heard from Grant. My heart sank. There was nothing to do but kick start the day with my daily kayak trip to greet Scratchy and friends. The afternoon went by quickly, and I was back on the Pali. I thought that perhaps Grant may have called the gym, so I couldn't wait to get to work. When I arrived, I found out my hunch was wrong, and I had a tough time staying focused on coaching. The team girls noticed my pensive mood and couldn't believe I wasn't constantly smiling and laughing with them. At the end of the day, I had no interest in free food or drinks and asked one of the coaches to give me a lift home. My gut said don't panic, and so I didn't. I went home and researched the Yukon. So desolate but also rich in culture. I learned much about the Gold Rush days and Calamity Kate! I made a cuppa and willed the phone to ring.

Finally, the phone rang. I sprang into action to answer and startled Sprite from her sleep so that she jumped straight up in the air on all fours. It was my boss letting me know about a schedule change for meets coming up the next month. I put down the receiver and resigned myself that I may have another night to wait. With that, I picked up the International Gymnastic magazine. Halfway through reading about Mary Lou Retton, an up-and-coming star, the phone rang. I calmly reached for the phone,

"Hello!" I answered pensively.

"Hey, Dizzy Izzy! It's Grant!" I could hear him smiling through the phone.

"I am so happy to hear from you. How was your trip?" I

asked with such excitement I had to put the phone down and jump up and down.

"We got delayed a few times. The plane into Whitehorse only flies in one time a day. If you miss it, you wait until the next day. We missed it. It's so great to hear your voice, Izzy."

"Yours too! I have been researching the Yukon! It sounds beautiful."

"Well, I have a surprise for you! I spoke to a director at the Whitehorse Hospital, and you are going to be getting a phone call from the human resource department tomorrow." Grant's words took me by surprise.

"Grant, did I hear you correctly? A person from the human resources at a hospital is going to call me for an interview?" I asked, speaking slowly to be sure there was no misunderstanding.

"Yes, yes! I told them about your background and speech pathology license, and they are in desperate need to fill an outreach position. Isn't that great! I told you I was going to marry you!"

"Wow, let's not get ahead of ourselves. I don't have certification in your country, and I haven't finished my fellowships and need three more years of clinical work to finish my medical doctorate. Don't get your hopes up," I quickly added.

"Nope! You are smart and well educated. I know they will want to hire you. Just do the interview. It is going to be at one p.m. because I told them you leave for work by two-thirty your time. They agreed even with the time change. The woman with whom you will be speaking to is named Veronica. She seemed really nice." Grant tried to persuade me soothingly.

"This is all a lot to take in, Grant. I will have to review and prep as it's been a while since I have spoken medical jargon!"

"You are going to be great. I am in love with you, and I know we can be happy together! I have to go now to train with the team, but please call me after the interview. I will wait for you tomorrow until I hear from you! I can't wait to find out when you are getting here!" Grant's rapid pace was enthusiastic and convincing. When I hung up the phone, I knew in my heart I would be with him soon.

That morning, I went kayaking early to clear my head. I played the game "let's suppose" with myself and ran through scenarios in my head. Did I work so hard to get where I was in judging and coaching to throw it all away? On the other hand, the thought of being with a person who would care about and cherish me was not too shabby either. After saying hello to my sea turtle friends, I paddled back to shore and had no more clarity than when I first got my toes wet earlier that morning. It was almost one p.m., and I was getting nervous. At precisely one p.m., the phone rang. I answered a bit too eagerly, "Hi, this is Isabella."

Hearing nothing on the other end, I repeated my greeting and said, "Hello, hello." Finally, I heard a female voice on the other end, "Hello, we may have a bad connection. This is Veronica calling from Whitehorse, Yukon."

"Yes, yes. I was expecting your call," I affirmed.

"Okay! Let me tell you a little bit about our program and then I will ask you a few questions," Veronica said.

"Great. I am not sure what Grant told you, but I hope you know that I haven't completed my fellowships yet," I offered.

"Yes, I checked and found you have a speech and language pathology license in the U.S., so that's good enough for me. We need an outreach worker who is licensed in several areas."

"Oh, oh, I see," I interjected.

"We are more than happy to pay for any additional coursework or fellowship experience you need. We also will provide you with survival workshops," Veronica answered.

"Survival?" I stammered.

"Yes, don't worry about it. A minor thing. You know, shooting a rifle, staying alive in minus fifty degree Celsius temps, dealing with bears, avalanches – the usual here. Nothing out of the ordinary." Veronica went on a bit more about the outreach programs and position requirements.

"Wow! It's a lot to take in. One thing you haven't mentioned was the salary range," I gingerly inquired.

"Oh, I am sorry, I didn't even think to mention it." Veronica laughed nervously. "The range is $60-$70,000 a year. I imagine the board would give you the upper end as we definitely have a need to fill the spot ASAP. The board will also pay for moving expenses and your visa application. So, what are your thoughts?"

"It all sounds great. I need a few days to think about it. If I accept, when do you need me to start?" I asked

"As soon as you can get here. The sooner the better. Shall we say I will call back in two days at one p.m. again for your answer?" Veronica quickly offered.

With hopes of conveying a genuine interest in the position, I responded with a firm "Yes! That would be perfect. In the meantime, I will do a little research about the area."

With that, we said goodbye, and I slowly placed the phone on the receiver. I promised to call Grant when I got back from coaching. Sitting on the bus going down the Pali, my head was swirling with scenarios. Somewhere deep inside, I knew that I would be saying goodbye to my coaching career and moving forward by taking a big girl job. Who was I kidding? The money was more than I could make in ten more years of coaching, and I knew I wanted to be with Grant.

Thankfully, routines went smoothly on all apparatus, and I

was on my way back home to call Grant. Sprite greeted me with head butts and sweet meows. Sprite fed, I dialed Grant's number. He must have been anxiously waiting as before I could hear the ringer, Grant was saying hello. "Well, Izzy, tell me everything."

I gave Grant a quick summary of the job description, salary, and benefits package.

"Izzy! That's incredible. I knew you were meant to be with me. So, when are you coming?"

"Well, Grant, I – I just have to think about it. I haven't said yes to Veronica. It's a lot to take in."

"Look, I want you here, and there is even a gymnastics team you can coach when you get here. They would love to have someone with your expertise. Everything is working out, so when are you coming?"

"I know, but it all sounds crazy! I barely know you. I have had my share of heart breaks so if I take the job, it's for me and not because I am getting swept off my feet by some man I barely know," I lied.

"Agreed. So, when are you coming? When will you tell your boss? The sooner you confirm the deal with Veronica, the better. I think you should get a used car and drive it up to Washington and cross into Canada over that border."

"What? Get a car? Drive where? This is getting a bit complicated!" I gasped.

"No, no. I can help you with the car. I can't wait until you get here, Izzy." Grant's words were reassuring and made me feel like I was wrapped in a warm, soft blanket on a cold night.

"Well, I have got to get some sleep. Talk tomorrow?" I offered.

"Absolutely! Let's chat at the same time. I can't wait to hear when you will be driving to Washington!" Grant repeated with enthusiasm.

Hanging up the phone, it seemed impossible that over a year had gone by living in Hawaii. It also seemed unlikely that I would have met a handsome Canadian hockey player who had fallen head over heels and managed to get me a job making five times what I was already making. With the information swirling in my mind like a shaken snow globe, I tried to sleep. Tossing and turning, I tried to fight every pore of my body screaming at me, "Go to Canada!" but it was impossible. There was no denying that I was going to talk to Leone in the morning.

Morning came, and I felt as if I were still dreaming about the events that happened the day before. I told myself to mull things over, follow my heart, and the words would come naturally when talking to Leone. The ocean seemed bluer, the sea turtles greener, my work out better, and my smoothie more delicious than ever. On the bus, I rehearsed what I would say to Leone. I knew that once I told him I was leaving, my career coaching would be over. After getting off the bus, the rest of the day was a blur. Leone did not take the news well. I agreed to go to meets held on Maui and the Big Island over the next three weeks and then leave. The team girls were not to know until after their last meet. It would be hard to say goodbye to everyone, but my heart was guiding me, and I was listening.

The phone rang when I reached my apartment door. I knew it would be Grant. I recounted how the day went and gave him a date that I would be driving to Washington. Grant assured me that buying a decent car in the Yukon would be difficult, if not very expensive, and since I would need a car, driving to meet him at the border made the most sense. Grant did some digging and located a six-month-old Jeep at a dealership in Nevada. The plan was to fly to Nevada, pick up the Jeep, and drive to meet Grant at the border at Peace Arch Crossing, Vancouver, British Columbia. It all seemed so easy. After I hung up the phone with Grant, I was convinced Sprite and I were making the right choice. Grant was so thoughtful. He told me he would have a jacket for me as I had no warm clothes with me. I felt as if I was on auto pilot for the next few weeks. Every victory my team girls captured was bittersweet. Every kayak trip was more precious than the one before as I would most definitely miss my large-shelled friends. Two weeks before my departure date, my optional team won the national title. It was all I could have hoped. I worked hard with the team to hit that prestigious ranking, and in a week, I would be leaving to venture into a completely unknown.

Grant called every night except when I was away at meets. When I got back from team nationals, Grant must have detected a little sadness in my voice. "You know, Izzy, the Yukon will be a new adventure, and you will still be able to coach. These girls will actually appreciate you more than you can imagine."

"I know what you are saying is true, but I can't help to question if I am crazy sometimes. Don't you think?" I asked as sweetly as possible.

"Of course, moving here is going to be a big change. There is no denying that, but I know I want to marry you and love you."

"The good news is Yukoners speak English, so I won't have to learn a new language." I laughed lightly. Grant and I went over the route he had prepared by the Canadian Automobile Club that I received in the mail. I felt confident about the drive and knew I was up for the adventure.

The last week was full of goodbyes, speed dancer performances, and no regrets. Locking the front door for the last time, I walked down to the ocean to say my goodbyes. I was off to Nevada, where a Jeep would be waiting for me in the airport parking lot. I felt like a queen. Grant thought of everything and was doing all he could to take care of me. I deserved this kind of love, and I truly felt like the most fortunate woman in the world. Little did I know what I was getting myself into – but that was half the allure, and Grant's sexy maleness was the other half.

The plane touched down, and I had little trouble finding the JEEP parked in the D block in long-term parking. I located the key in the spare key magnetic case under the fender and opened the JEEP. It was a cherry red stick shift with fog lamps and plaid seats. First things first, I had to get a hotel room and go shopping for a few warm sweaters and a jacket. I knew going to a thrift store was my best chance at finding affordable apparel. I updated Grant with a quick phone call and, exhausted, fell asleep. I planned to drive ten hours the first day and get over Mount Shasta. Then the second day would be much easier. I turned the nightstand light off and fell asleep quickly. I felt absolutely positive this was the path my life was meant to take, and soon I would be living in the Yukon – for good or for bad.

The weather in Nevada was a balmy forty-five degrees Fahrenheit, and I told myself I could get used to colder weather. Sprite wasn't so sure about the cold, but he happily curled up on his soft faux fur blanket in his crate. He didn't seem to mind driving, and for that, I was grateful. Listening to a plethora of music genres, with every mile, it seemed to be getting colder. Getting gas and a hot chocolate, I noticed the tv in the store was showing the weather. "Excuse me, sir, but can you turn that up?"

The store clerk was amiable and turned the volume up in time for me to hear a snow storm was predicted on top of Mount Shasta. My face turned white, and an audible gasp escaped. "Hey ma'am, are you headed that way? It sure looks like a doozie. Do you have chains for your tires?"

"No, I think I will be fine. I have a JEEP that should get me through it," I nervously replied. "Don't you think?"

"Well, if it's a four-wheel drive. Otherwise, you may want to wait this out," the clerk suggested.

"No time for that! Wish me luck." I waved and smiled. It never occurred to me that I should be concerned. I had never driven in a snowstorm but did experience cold weather in college, and with a few snow days of driving, I felt I could conquer the upcoming mountain. "Okay, Sprite! There is going to be a big old snowstorm, so don't worry. We will be okay. I promise."

After another six hours, the weather became noticeably threatening. At the base of Mount Shasta, a few cars were pulling over, so I decided to do the same. A truck driver came over to Sprite and me and asked if I needed help putting on tire chains. Of course, I had no idea what the trucker was talking about or why my tires needed chains. After explaining I had just got the car and was driving to the Yukon and I had no chains, the truck driver tried persuading me to wait a few days. I was not having it. Nor could I reach Grant as he was on his way to meet me, and neither of us had a way to contact the other. I did not have a mobile car phone. So, despite the weather, I plodded on. My stomach was in knots, my hands gripped the steering wheel for dear life, and I tried to sing along to Salt N' Pepper to keep my nerves in check. Just when I thought Sprite and I might make it over the mountain, a terrible clunking noise, followed by a screech, came from the back axle of the Jeep. A light on the dashboard started flashing, and I pulled over. The snow was coming down quite steadily, and inches were piling up. I had no gloves, no hat or boots, and no idea what to do. I rummaged in the back of the trunk and found a flare. I managed to light it and place it in front of my car. I was cold – very cold – and terrified to run the car for heat as I didn't know what was wrong with the JEEP.

Huddled in the JEEP with Sprite on my lap, I put as many clothes as possible on top of both of us and asked the 'Spirits that Be' to help me out. Not many people came up the mountain, and I was losing hope. Finally, I heard a car coming close. The snow-covered windows made it hard to see, but the car lights were shining and coming closer. The JEEP's hazard lights were on, and the flare was nearing its end. My gut told me to get out of the car and flag the car down. By some miracle, the car stopped, and a man and a woman in their late thirties pulled over.

"Yes, well, let's not overstate the obvious," I said with nervous laughter. "There were some bangs and shrieks, and the car limped over to the side here. My cat and I are freezing!"

"Okay, well, no one is going to be able to come out and tow you to a service station in this weather. Where are you headed?" he asked.

"I am supposed to meet someone at the Washington-Vancouver border crossing tonight," I offered.

"Well, we are headed that way ourselves. My name is Rock – like it says on my shirt. I work for the border patrol, and this here is my wife, Lindsay. She works for the sheriff's department. Suppose you could come with us. You can't stay here and freeze to death."

Considering my options, I could only agree with him. Despite him looking like he and his wife just came out of the 'love child hippie era', I knew I had no choice. I was saved!

I secured the car on the side of the road and left a note with a phone number to call in the Yukon as well as my new friends' contact information. I took one suitcase and Sprite, and we piled into the half of the back seat that was empty. The couple seemed pleasant enough, and then they started smoking a joint. I was terrified that I would never make it to the border and that we would be pulled over for illegal drug use. I tried to cover my nerves by chatting endlessly with the two strangers who were my salvation. The minutes turned into hours. Sleep eluded me. Finally, I spied a green sign saying "Vancouver Border, Peace Arch Crossing 100 miles." My heart filled with hope and happiness. It is going to be okay, I thought, stroking Sprite's head. The inside of the car was pungent with pot smoke, but I was appreciative of the warmth and moving forward.

"Only a hundred more miles. I can't believe it!" I said to Sprite. Lindsay, completely pot-baked, whooped and clapped for me, "Isabella, you are close to your happily ever after!" Her words were filled with joy and excitement for me. I started to sweat when we got nearer to the border. At that moment, I reached for my passport and job confirmation letter and could find neither. I began to panic. It was still dark, so I had to ask Rock to put on the interior lights. I looked in every rucksack pocket and zippered pouch and found nothing. I nervously took out everything from my rucksack and suitcase. Nothing. I was panic-stricken!

"Lindsay, I left my passport and employment letter in the JEEP! All I have is a license that says Hawaii. What am I going to do? What do I say to the Border Patrol?" I asked with a shaky voice denoting terror.

"Don't worry about it, Izzy. It will be okay. As soon as Rock gives his license and they find out he works for Border Patrol, it will be no problem."

My heavy breathing and face of distress must have conveyed the depth of terror I was feeling. Lindsay again assured me and told me that no matter what, just agree with what they say. "Don't speak up or offer any information unless they directly ask you a question. Okay?" Lindsay informed me.

Being silent when I felt this nervous was going to be a tall order, but I prepared myself for the next forty-five minutes. Finally, we got to the border, and it was our turn. I stayed in the back seat with sweat taking over my entire body. Praying to myself, I waited quietly.

Rock rolled down his window. "How are you today, Officer?"

"Where are you headed, sir? Your license please."

Horrified by this officer's straight-laced attitude and business face, I held my breath. The officer looked at Lindsay and asked for her identification. I heard Lindsay say, "Hello officer, I am headed to the correctional facility in Vancouver. I'm Sergeant Lindsay. Hope your day has been a good one."

The officer glanced at me in the back. Sprite was quiet, and I prayed he would not make a peep. I covered Sprite's cage with a blanket to keep him warmer, and luckily the officer didn't notice the crate. He took Lindsay's paperwork and asked Rock if everyone in the car was a U.S. Citizen. Rock shook his head and confidently said, "Yes, sir." And with that, we were waved onward to Vancouver. At the welcome center, I thanked my two unlikely heroes, gathered my two bags and Sprite, and found a table by the window to look out for Grant. I knew he had a red truck and that he should be arriving a few hours later than I. The trip was an ordeal, and I could only hope I would not be waiting long. With that, I bought a book in the welcome center on the Yukon Territory. I honestly had no idea what I was getting into, but that didn't matter. I was ready to be with Grant, and there was no turning back now. While reading that cars had to be plugged in due to the extreme car temperatures, I felt someone come up behind me.

"What a site for sore eyes," Grant said empathetically. He picked me up by the waist and hugged me and hugged me! The relief flooded my body, and I had no words. "Izzy, I can't believe it. You are here! I am so happy. And let's not forget Sprite. Hey, little kitty." Sprite gave Grant a quiet meow. We hugged again and again.

"Izzy, I booked a hotel room, so let's go get some sleep and we will start fresh in the morning. We will have 21:32 hour drive ahead of us. So, let's get a good night's sleep. We will deal with the Jeep once we get to the Yukon. I already called a service station near Mt. Shasta, and they will be towing the car to their shop tomorrow."

"Oh my God! You are amazing! You have thought of everything! Let's get a hot shower and some sleep. I also just realized I am hungry. With all that happened, I didn't even think of eating these past eight hours!"

Grant had some cheese muffins in his truck. "I don't think there is anything open at this hour. It's almost one a.m., but these are really good. A friend made them for me for the trip."

Biting into the cheese muffin, I saw the motel ahead. I knew I had made the right decision. I was going to be a Yukoner. I was so exhausted that I didn't even feel awkward about sleeping next to Grant. His warm body and well-sculpted muscles said, "Welcome home" to me. With that, I fell fast asleep safe in Grant's arms. He nuzzled his nose between my shoulders, and I felt at home. The tenderness mixed with the fierce but glorious physicality of Grant made my body blush with happiness. With the morning came a blast of frigid air. The reality of leaving ninety degree weather with warm island breezes began to assault me as I opened the hotel door to the February freeze of

Vancouver. It was thirty degrees, and my bones and body were stiff and begging for exercise to warm up. "Hey Izzy, you are up early." Grant extended his arm, beckoning me to join him. I tumbled into the bed, expertly performing a forward roll and landing my head purposefully on his chest. Grant planted soft kisses as if to tease me, and I didn't want to break the spell he had upon me. "Okay, Dizzy Izzy. We have a long day, and we will probably hit some patches of snow along the way. I brought you some moose hide muck lucks and beaver fur mittens. You are going to need them."

"Grant, these gloves and boot thingies are gorgeous with the beading. They smell like animals, and the fur is so soft. It seems so mean to have killed an animal so I can be warm."

"The meat was eaten by the family, and you won't be thinking about how the moose or beaver felt once you greet the below zero temps. Trust me, Izzy. I will take care of you." Grant smiled proudly, displaying his hockey war wound. I couldn't believe how such a viral manly man had such a kind, sensitive side. "He's mine! He's mine!" I screamed silently in my head as I imagined the energizer bunny running back and forth, beating his drum.

"Izzy, we are loaded and ready to go."

I smiled, and Grant picked me up to the truck bench seat. "Here we go. You will officially become a Cheechako in another thirty-two hours."

"Oh, I didn't realize it was so far. It will give us lots of time to get to know each other. My first question is, where's your passenger side windshield wiper?" I couldn't help but just stare at this Greek God of a man. My face hurt from non-stop smiling and gazing while listening to stories about the Yukon moose, elk, bison, porcupines, and bears. For once, I was a listener, and Grant had my full attention. I learned he had ten brothers and sisters and was born a Yukoner. His father tried his hand at gold mining but with little success. I also learned Grant and I shared a violent childhood and parental estrangement. However, he was bitter and hated his father for the abuses directed against his mother. I, on the other hand, had not spoken to my parents since I was fifteen and had not seen my siblings. Grant was very happy with his brothers and sisters. I learned he owned a mechanical engineering company as well as playing hockey for a living. Could life get any better than this?

Chapter 18

Taking in the sights of frozen blue ice hanging from mountain cliffs, the Yukon River, the staunchly dry bitter cold air, and the spotty bits of life that were the town, I came face to face with my new world – my new adventure. When the red truck, now worse for wear, pulled into the city of Whitehorse, it never occurred to me to even ask Grant if he lived in a house, condo complex, an apartment, or a log cabin. How a tiny detail escaped my curiosity, I had no idea, but the mystery was solved when we pulled into a small plot of land that had a single, wide trailer. "Well, here we are! Home sweet home! It's not much, Izzy. But it's ours!" Grant beamed with pride. "Let's get you and Sprite acquainted with your new home!"

I had never been in a trailer home, and I never thought I would be living in one; however, this minor detail did not dissuade nor deter the admiration I had for Grant. It was clear that the only important luxuries in this land was having a heater, a place to plug in the car in front of your home, and warm, indigenous accessories to keep the limbs from frostbite. The outdated paneling, olive green wallpaper, dark brown cloth bulky furniture, and overall décor of the home screamed man cave, but it was all fixable. Looking out of the trailer's front bay window, the view was spectacular – Mount Sumanik to the northwest, Golden Horn Mountain to the south, and Grey Mountain to the east. The majestic mountainside grabbed my heart and soul. I quickly became grateful for the warmth and solitude of my new home. Sprite, on the other hand, was not as keen as I.

The first night in my new home, Sprite and I were bedazzled by the stars. The sky lit up like Christmas lights as no light pollution existed over the mountains. The first night, Grant lit candles and introduced me to the Klondike Bar – restaurant – nightclub – gossip hut, where we ordered the best Asian chicken wings I had ever tasted. Because Whitehorse is a very small town, and, further, Grant was a born and raised Yukoner, most of the men in town came to check out the "American – Australian Girlie". I danced endlessly into the night, the entire time wanting to feel the sweet touch of Grant covering my body. After a few rounds of shots, Grant and I could no longer wait to be alone. Leaving the Klondike, the Northern Lights showered the sky with radiant beauty that I had never yet experienced.

The night could not have been more magical. Back home, the car safely plugged in, and Sprite snuggled in his bed, Grant lit vanilla-scented candles and opened a bottle of champagne. "To us, Izzy. I am so happy you are here." With those words, Grant touched my face with such tenderness that I forgot it was thirty below zero! Grant scooped me up in his arms and carried me to the bedroom. Every sense in my body was awakened. Every touch, every kiss, and every sweet nothing whispered in my ear led to feeling the most naked I had ever felt. Grant embodied sex in his movements, smile, and touch. The level of intimacy brought Grant and me to an emotional high like no other. I was Grant's – completely and fully – my heart belonged to Grant.

The first morning I opened my eyes as a resident of Whitehorse, I had no regrets about leaving my coaching world behind. I was in love with a man who satiated my every desire. Grant was funny, practical, exceedingly kind, a bit hard-headed, and very athletic. He knew how to cook better than I and didn't mind doing it. I had two days before embarking on my new career in medicine, so after a cuppa hot tea and omelet, I was ready for sight seeing. Our trailer was a few miles outside of the capital city, Whitehorse, where I would be working. With one stop light in town and one main highway, the city was not difficult to navigate. The tour of the town lasted fifteen minutes. It was clear I would be saving money as the one general store and grocery store in town did not scream Gucci and Gabbana. For the remainder of the days before work commenced, Grant shared his life's work as a hockey player, a gold miner, and a bridge builder. He also shared his virile manhood in all its glory.

Learning to get up early was not as easy as I expected. I was not a great "getter upper" as I had been living a coach's life, which never required me to get up early. The getting up part, I knew, was going to be tough. Luckily, Grant had a second car other than the truck – a Shelby – which was his pride and joy. I preferred to drive the truck, but it was getting repaired, so I had no choice but to get my "snow legs" with a fast car that did not take to ice or snow very well. A bit frazzled after fishtailing in the car a few times, I managed to park the car, plug it in, and get my dithers about me as I pushed through the front door of the hospital. Preparing to meet my new boss, Veronica, my nerves were on edge.

Within moments, Veronica came flying into the lobby. She was tall, confident, and authoritative when she walked toward me. "Hello, it's nice to meet you face to face after all our phone calls! Welcome to Whitehorse."

"G'day! Thank you! It's nice to put a face to a voice as well! I didn't realize I was going to need sunnies in the frozen tundra." I laughed lightly.

"Sunnies?" Veronica said with amusement.

"Oh, sorry, habit. My sunglasses. I was practically blinded coming down Wann Road into the city from the sun bouncing off the snowy mountains."

"Well, you will get used to it. Actually, today after completing your paperwork, you will be meeting your partner in crime, Susan, who will go with you every other week on the outreach trips."

"Great! I can't wait to get started. I did have a little hiccup coming as you may have heard from Grant. I will have to take a few days off to retrieve the JEEP in the States, so I am sure you can tell me when it is best on the calendar to plan that trip in the very near future."

"Oh yes, I heard! That sounded like some adventure. Glad you are safe and here now."

Veronica and I completed never-ending pages of immigration paperwork, employment and government documents, and a tour throughout the hospital. Numerous introductions to staff and colleagues rounded out the morning. During a late afternoon tea break, my request to Veronica to call my brother in Asia and my sister in the States was granted with a bit of coolness from Veronica. It wasn't until a few weeks later that I learned why. It never occurred to me that a phone call could be so expensive. The very first phone bill Grant received after my arrival was $687.00. Evidently, the Yukon phone lines required very expensive maintenance, or I had a lot to say to friends when we spoke. Either way, I quickly learned that phone calls had to be short and sweet at work and home.

Susan turned out to be an earthy, outspoken, kind woman who was ten years my senior. Luckily, we hit it off instantly, and my worry about working so closely with a traveling co-worker quickly abated. Prior to our first road trip, I took survival courses.

I learned how to survive with a single candle in desolate, frigid conditions. I also learned that carrying extra petrol containers was essential if we were going to make it back as there were no petrol stations from point A to point B.

The first outreach road trip brought as many unexpected wonders and delights as it did unexpected poverty and illness in the villages and towns serviced. I routinely saw dahl sheep, muskox, elk, moose, bears, and grouse. I clapped every time. I called Grant every evening from the village medical center satellite phone in our visiting doctor apartment that myself and Susan called our temporary home. I didn't think I would ever get accustomed to the sharp, almost painful, freezing of my nares and nasal hairs when stepping outside in below zero temperatures. But winter was only ten months a year, I told myself. Eventually, the twenty-four-hour sun would make an entrance, and I would tee off at the golf course at two or three a.m. I would be off to enjoy the short four weeks of summer.

The language of the indigenous tribes was glottal and guttural, much like the West Australian aboriginal dialect. In a very odd way, I felt as if my soul had lived in the Yukon all these years. The overwhelming quietness kissed my insides with a peace I had never known. And then there was Grant. A magnificent specimen of a man and a human being.

In my third week in Whitehorse, I was introduced to the local Whitehorse gymnastics club. At first, I felt I shouldn't jump in and save the blossoming gymnasts who lacked coaching expertise, a proper facility, replacement of antiquated equipment, and cohesiveness as a team. However, I was persuaded my expertise would be welcomed with open arms, and I needed them as much as they needed me. The gymnasts were not fine-tuned athletes, but they had a lot of heart. I managed to put together a lower-level compulsory and optional team. The girls gave their all when I was in the gym and showed progress. Our first meet was scheduled in Alaska three months after I joined the coaching team. I was excited to take the ferry to Juneau and could not wait to see the great Orca and humpback whales I had heard so much about. The ferry trip did not disappoint, and a pod of humpback whales graced the waters several times on the journey. The majestic gracefulness of the whales must have been an omen. We returned triumphant as silver medal winners.

When Grant met me at the dock in Skagway to pick me up, his face told me the victory party had to wait. "Hey, Izzy, I am so proud of you!" he said, trying to hide his worry. Sitting in the red truck with a repaired windshield wiper and new windshield, Grant's silence was atypical and worrisome.

"Okay, what's going on? I can tell you don't want to tell me something." It seemed as if the silence was endless.

"A friend of yours called. She said her name was Sandie. Somehow, she was contacted by a man claiming to be your uncle. Sandie said to call her back as soon as possible. Whatever is going on, it doesn't sound good, Izzy. You never talk about your family, so just know I am here if you need me."

"My uncle?" I asked, turning my eye to gaze at the mountain tops. I have not thought of Danny in years and wondered if something had happened to him. I instantly regretted not reaching out to him after our roommate disaster. But life has no play book and to date I often was clumsy when executing life's plans. This was the first time Grant and I didn't chat endlessly while on a road trip. A few hours later, the truck pulled up to the trailer. "You should call Sandie before it's too late. Don't worry about how long you talk." Grant winked and retrieved my suitcase. Sprite gleefully meowed to welcome me home from Alaska. The warmth of the trailer felt good. I reached for the phone, not sure what to expect.

"Hey Sandie. How are you? What's going on? Grant said you got a strange phone call from an uncle of mine?"

Sandie explained that our old boss at the Sunpapers in Maryland called trying to find me and that our old boss gave the person Sandie's number as the best contact for me. Clearly, this someone had no idea that I had left years prior. After Sandie updated me on her life and my godchild's, she spoke emphatically, "Izzy, I would call!"

"I suppose you are right, Sandie. I will fill you in when I find out."

"Okay, well you can just email me. I am sure you don't want another $700 phone bill." We both laughed as we hung up. Number in hand, I knew in this situation, a Mom "D" "don't put off tomorrow what you can do today," saying was in order.

The phone was ringing, and part of me hoped this was all a mistake. When the voice on the other end answered, I felt gut-punched. The voice had a manly pitch and cadence I had long forgotten that was hauntingly eerie. "Hello, is someone there? Who is this?" the voice asked.

Gathering my courage, I managed a weak reply. "Oh, I'm here. G'day. This is Isabella. My friend Sandie gave me this number, but I am not sure why," I stammered.

Confusion seemed to befuddle me when I realized the voice on the other end of the line was asking me if I was the youngest Notski daughter. My heart pounded uncontrollably. I felt flush as if I would faint at any moment. "No, no," I thought to myself. I would not let anyone take away the peace I had found in my new Yukon heaven. The voice kept saying the word "Grandmother" as if this *was* a word I used frequently in conversation. Then the voice began wavering a bit and said the funeral arrangements would be next week. Shell-shocked, I hung up the phone without saying goodbye.

My bubble burst, and the beast of reality came beckoning. Grant watched as I stood glued to the space I occupied, speechless and off-kilter. "Izzy, are you okay? What happened? Your brother? Sister?"

I could barely mumble the words, "No...paternal grandmother died."

Grant's reaction mirrored my face of bewilderment. For the first time in the short few months that we were together, he didn't know what to do to comfort me. Hell, I didn't think I needed any comforting. My unease was not because of the death of the grandmother I hardly recalled meeting only a few times as a toddler, but the fact that someone in my family found a way to contact me. That was the most disturbing. How dare they search where their tentacles were unwarranted – unwanted. I was devoid of emotion until fear struck from deep within. Fear seared through every nerve ending until my eyes blurred with the well of empty, voiceless tears. Not tears over losing a second grandmother, but tears that reminded me I am a product of such a fractured, dysfunctional lineage. Worse – the thought of my parents being there terrified me. No, I would not let *her* creep into my life to undermine and destroy the identity I had built. Then, in one split second of clarity, I knew I had to go. I had to spear the dragon and not allow *her* – my mother – to keep me captive for the remainder of my life's journey.

Looking at Grant, I knew there was no escaping the years of pain and scars I had carried unless I conquered my fear. I would go to say goodbye to a woman I barely knew, but whose death may bring answers that could give me peace. This scenario felt like a replay – but I would not be sucked into a false hope of finding a Norman Rockwell family portrait awaiting me. I was ready to quell my demons, but not *that* ready. My life was perfect and filled with Grant's love. With great strength and caution, I permitted myself to believe that perhaps, just perhaps, there was love of family out there for me. I was the eternal optimist. I had to try.